one man's place

one man's place

JOHN F DEANE

POOLBEG

Published in 1994 by
Poolbeg,
A division of Poolbeg Enterprises Ltd,
Knocksedan House,
123 Baldoyle Industrial Estate,
Dublin 13, Ireland

© John F Deane 1994

The moral right of the author has been asserted.

A catalogue record for this book is available from the British Library.

ISBN 1 85371 348 1

Cover painting *Redbrick but not a Game* by Camille Souter reproduced with the kind permission of the Trustees of the Ulster Museum
Cover design by Poolbeg Group Services Ltd/Bite Design
Set by Poolbeg Group Services Ltd in Garamond 10/13
Printed by The Guernsey Press Company Ltd,
Vale, Guernsey, Channel Islands.

The Publishers gratefully acknowledge the support of

The Arts Council / An Chomhairle Ealaíon.

ON ANOTHER SHORE

The worn-out Otherthing
rigid on its slab, the fluids
stagnant;
dressed up and parcelled – the Offence;

someone had set a plastic rose
upon the chest,
and we, attendants,
faces unmasked by grief,

murmured our studied words :
he is not dead, but sleeping,
he is not here,
he has stepped out on another shore

beautiful beyond belief;
and we have crept back out
into weakened sunshine,
knowing our possibilities

diminished.

ONE

DAVID

THE PHONE RANG AT PRECISELY SIX O'CLOCK THIS MORNING, jerking me out of sleep. I was instantly awake. As if, somewhere within the dark folds of my sleeping and dreaming, I knew the call was coming, and I was ready for it.

"Good morning."

"Good morning. Is that Blakes? Mr David Blake?"

When the phone rings at such times there is scarcely need to answer it. You know what it means. You reach in behind the calm, professional voice, to find the real words.

"It's your father, it's about your father ... "

When we arrived at the hospital he barely opened his eyes to see us. I suppose there was some instant of recognition but he gave no sign. His breathing is frightful, he's propped up in bed but looks as if he could collapse any moment, fall sideways, out of the bed onto the floor. I hated the five decades of the rosary we rattled out at him. I wonder if he can hear us. If he can, the prayers must sound terrible to him, a message, a threat, we're praying for your soul, pray for us sinners now and at the hour ...

The words, perhaps, are a way of saying something. I want to hold that old, scarred hand, soothe the restless, shifting head, tell him so much that I never did tell him. About so much. But I can't do that. I'm not able to. And I'm not so sure he'd want me to. He's proud. Above all don't break down, don't yield to it, don't cry. That was him, always. Know your place and hold it, he'd say, hold it and be proud of it.

Now that hand, where he lies on the hospital bed, rises often to his face, restlessly, rubbing as if to cleanse himself, as if to wipe something away from his flesh. As if to wash away the world. Eyes closed. Breathing terrible. I cry for him. And for myself. Where do we go from here? Where, where on earth do we go from here?

Northwards the rain
washes grey over the world; westwards
distance, black impasto clouds;
in a blunt Ford Prefect

smelling of oiled upholstery, tobacco, must,
I hold the big, moulded, driving wheel;
around us the island sandybanks,
the obstacles are sheep,

streams, and hare-track culverts;
the future is there, beyond the dashboard,
out over the bonnet, a huge,
a virgin canvas. Father,

straight-backed, fleshed out with tenderness,
holds my fingers on the wheel;
noon, and stillness, the first day;
he is gazing out the rear window

over sand-dunes, an ochre strand, the sea,
the skin of his face
finger-applied out of limed clay;
God's image, in waistcoat

and grey collarless shirt,
the white stud dangling. Still
life. And far away, in the background,
a milk-white gannet dives into the sea.

Matthew

If i lie perfectly still i can hold the pain at bay. Hold my body stiff as a tree. Like a capital letter; like the "I".

Every movement is agony. Every breath I draw, heave in out of the world and force down into my lungs, is a suffering to me.

Night is worst of all. I do not seem to have slept for years. The pain in my chest is a source of fire to my whole body. I was rigid all night. Rigid as a plank. A heavy branch, falling.

They are sitting by the bed, watching. Suffering, too. I cannot acknowledge their presence. My eyelids are too heavy. I cannot lift them.

I have no hope of speaking. Words are stones lodged in the thick mud of my mouth. In the pocket of my dressing-gown is my pen; slim, silver, Parker, almost too svelte to be held between my thickened fingers. The words came out of it like those shivering, oil-coated cormorants in the Gulf, thin and unsteady and dying; even my name, Matthew Robert Blake, in these last weeks, whenever I tried to write it, came staggering off the pen, small, quivering, trailing away.

Even lying perfectly still, hauling hand over hand at my breathing, the pain will catch me out. I can hear myself then. A cry that escapes from me, against my will. A small scream of protest against the mechanisms of the turning world.

The first suggestion that light was coming from outside was a source of relief to me. Night would be over. If not soon – because the word soon has lost all meaning for me – at least I knew the turn towards it had begun. Day would come. Pain is more supportable in the light. A ward at night is a battlefield. None of us slept. We were fighting for breath. How the mind hurt. How I missed the touch of her hand. Even the passing of her breathing near me would have been something. A lightening of my burden. An easing of the weight. Perhaps ...

If I were to force my eyes open I might glimpse her. At the side of the bed. At the foot ... It will have to be a slow, short opening. It hurts. Like lifting a weight while there is pain down along the spine. The attempt. For a moment ... Aaagh! ...

Only pain. And foolishness! She's dead. She has been dead for four years. How can I be so foolish? Above all the mind must not go. What I have to face I must face with all my powers. She is dead. And today ...

Today, the twenty-third of February, nineteen ninety-one. 23/2/1991. A date. Numbers. Figures. Marks, signalling events on the huge wheel. 23/2/91. Momentous. I often wondered what my figures would be. Now these are mine. Given to my name. Concluding figures. Now for ever. Whatever that *for ever* may mean. And today they are to begin war in the desert. It will be a good day to abandon this world. I am tired of it, tired, tired, tired.

Big Con Rohan was the first. His red hair scalped about his

ears and the nape of his neck, lifting and thrusting forward over his forehead like a fist. He blew it back out of his eyes every so often, curling his lower lip so he could blow upwards out of the side of his mouth. I feared him even while I despised him with my whole soul.

Kerry. Kerry. My place! Behind the low schoolhouse in Drumdouglas there was a stream running between the schoolyard and Shanahan's field. It was a wet place, cramped with fuchsia bushes, whitethorn hedges, rushes, furze. There were patches of wet grass, wet scutch-covered mounds and hillocks. The schoolroom wall was a blank; wet brick with green slime from a broken chute, and a rusty, excremental brown climbing upwards from the ground. I was in second class, Con in fifth.

It was lunchtime. I took my sandwich and wandered behind the school to be alone. I found Con, big, burly, red-haired Con, rooting among the thorn bushes by the ditch. He saw me and called me over. He had found a nest, a greenfinch's nest, I could see it, built and hidden with perfection deep inside the hedge. Con was perched in amongst the branches and was handing me the eggs.

"Here, Matt, take these carefully, let you. Put them down on the soft grass and the moss. They're great. There's three of them. Take them, let you, quickly."

"It's wrong to take the bird's eggs, Con. Put them back."

"Here, take them, you bloody eejit. Take them, quick. I'm just about holding on here. Take them."

"I won't, Con, I don't want to. You'll destroy the nest. The birds will never come back."

Con turned and eyed me. I can still see the question and the anger in that awful eye.

"Take them from me, now, Matt, or by God I'll make you suffer."

I stood still, chewing on the crusty bit of my sandwich. We were both bare-footed, it was Spring, and I could see the way his large, white feet curled around a low branch. His knees were red and blotchy; he wore brown corduroy trousers, a green jumper. We looked at each other. I did not stir.

"Right," he said, "you just wait till I get out to you."

He tossed one of the lovely, small eggs towards a grassy patch. He missed, the egg smashed; splosssht! I could see the dark-brown huddled shape in the green mucous that spilled onto the ground. It was the most vulnerable thing I had ever seen, lost already, curled in upon itself, pulsating.

"Now look what you've done," I shouted at him, "the bird was ready to be hatched. You're horrible. It's a sin, what you've done, it's a sin, I know it."

Con said nothing. Still holding on with his feet and one hand he reached towards the nest for another egg. I had to do something. I flung my sandwich at his flaming red hair and hit him on the back of the head. He was so startled he lost his grip and fell back through the thorns onto the ditch. He yelled with pain as thorns gashed his knees, his wrists, his feet, and he fell heavily onto the grass.

I was a fool; I gloated.

Con picked himself up, looking at the pricks of blood on his flesh. He was punished, I felt, for his crimes; two more greenfinches would be born, their soft green plumage and the bright yellow bands on wing and tail would grow and develop, they would flash through the dullness of our hedgerows like smiles across a saddened face.

Con brushed himself off, glaring at me, determined and ugly. He paused, looked towards the broken egg with the pathetic foetus, then stepped towards it and crushed it down into the earth, stomping on it with one big, bare foot, watching me, curling and uncurling his great, red fists.

"There's your bird for you, you little bugger. That's what

I think of you, too. And I'll be back for the others. You wait and see. First, though, it's your turn."

He came rushing at me with a violence before which I could do nothing but collapse. He punched me hard, in the stomach; all my breath burst out of me and I jerked forward and bent almost double, gasping; he caught me around the neck, my head in under his armpit, and he squeezed, hard, hard, hard. I could not breathe, I wanted to scream for air but no sound came from my mouth; it was awful; then he threw me onto the wet grass and leaped onto me; he was kneeling on my stomach, punching me on the chest, on the arms, on the face, anywhere he could reach, his face purple under the carrot red of his hair, ugly, ugly, ugly.

I was hurt, crying, I kept my hands up in front of my face. His knees were grinding into me, I could feel the wetness from the ground seeping through the clothes along my back.

Big Con grew tired. He got up off his knees and straddled my chest, sitting on me, letting his weight drop onto me. Again my breathing became a gasping effort as he sat, looking down on me. He was at least three, maybe four years older than me; he was much bigger and heavier than I was. He was crushing me. I had the feeling that my chest would collapse under his weight; the way the bone-flesh of a beetle will crunch under the weight of a human foot; each breath I took I had to lift his weight to allow space in my lungs. Just like now. The pain. Only now it's as if Big Con were inside my chest, straining to get out.

He was quieter, looking down at me. I knew he was beginning to assess the possibilities of having to present some sort of explanation to the Master.

"Matt," he said, quietly, as if all his anger had evaporated. "You're a bugger. It's all your fault. And I'm bloody well not getting into trouble because of you. So we're going to agree on something. Now, before the whistle goes."

Those were the scarlet days of Master Brosnan, a small, elderly man with a sudden heart and a sudden hand. I was a good scholar and had no problems learning from him. But I feared him, as we all did, his quick decisions, his murderous punishing.

Con was thinking. "So, young Matt," he said, "this is what you tell the Master. It was you was climbing in the bushes, looking for birds' nests. It was you found the greenfinch's nest, and you fell, the drain got you wet and dirty, the fall bloodied your nose. Right? I wasn't even here. That's the story. You'll have to tell the Master. Or I'll get you again, and I swear to God that I'll break you. I'll blacken you. I'll break each of your fingers, slowly, one after the other."

Big Con opened the fly on his corduroy trousers. He took out his penis, soft, like a fat, swollen grub, like a prawn, shelled, the little slit at the end of it brown and threatening. He sat higher up on my chest, almost on my neck, and he waved his penis about over my face.

"Swear it!" he said, "swear it! or I'll piss all over you."

How could I swear to a lie? It would be terrible, a lie! and swearing to it. I was terrified, unable to bear the thought of another beating, of having my fingers broken.

"Wait," I said to him, "wait. I can't swear to a lie. But I swear I won't mention you at all. I won't tell. I swear I won't tell."

"That's not enough!" he hissed down at me, "he'll force you to tell him something, and I know you, you'll tell on me. I know you will. So you'll swear, now! What I said."

Again he moved that ugly grub above me; he held it tight, then, and I could see it swell slightly, and straighten, the slit opened, and a tiny jet of his urine burst down onto my face.

"There!" he said, "that's just a start. To show you I'm serious. Swear!"

I was crying. "I swear," I said, "I swear. I won't tell on you. I swear I won't mention your name. I swear it. But I can't swear to tell a lie. I can't do that, Con, please Con, I can't do that."

"You little bugger you!" he said, and he raised himself above me and urinated all over my face. I closed my eyes tight, and my mouth, and suffered it. Suffered the lukewarm, sharpsmelling evil stuff to gush over me. It was nothing. It would end. I could wash it all away from me. But I don't suppose I did, I can remember it, even now, as if it had happened half an hour ago. Big Con, and the seeping of moisture up through my clothes from the ground, and the little brown flesh huddled in its mucous, tiny shards of egg-shell clinging to it, never, never, never have I wiped all that away from me ...

Oh they were heady days! I would be master of all knowledge, I would ride the world, build cities, make my soul a bright jewel in the Lord's crown! Who made the world? God made the world. And who is God? God is the creator and sovereign Lord of Heaven and Earth and of all things. Sing-song singalong, ding dong bell!

Master Brosnan, I remember his glee the day he filled the classroom with white lilies, the swan-like rise of them, the large, green perfection of the leaves with their sheen; that long, pollen-rich tongue that reached from the flower into the stale air of our classroom.

"Down on your knees, boys, down I say, and pray to God and the great patriots who have walked amongst us, who have taken their places with the saints of Heaven, beside St Patrick and St Brigid and St Colmcille, beside Tone and Emmet and Father Murphy, giving their life's blood for Ireland. Down boys, down, down now, and pray!"

And the songs we sang, freedom songs, full of blood and sacrifice, rippling with the muscle of their martial airs. We had pictures of Mother Ireland on the walls, we called her all her secret names, singing them out for the Master, our Little Drom Dilis, our Dark Rosaleen, our Fodhla, our Erin …

Master Brosnan strode the classroom in a frenzy of delight.

"Great days, boys, great, holy days. You are going to take your place among the nations of the earth, bring the truth and purity of the Catholic faith out of Ireland once again and into the pagan nations of the world. Irish, boys, ye are Irish, ye are free, the first to take your places as free men of Ireland. Look at ye! a bunch of clodhoppers and barnacle pickers and seaweed eaters! what am I supposed to do with ye at all at all at all!" and he laughed his great, yellow-orange laugh that warmed our hearts with optimism for the day.

"Blake! For God's own sake man, what happened to you at all? Up, man, up, and let me have a look at you."

I stood, wet, cut, bleeding. I folded my hands in front of my crotch and I bowed my head.

"I fell, sir, in the ditch, in the thorns."

"You did, boy, and what were you doing in the ditch, in the thorns?"

"Exploring, sir."

"Exploring, were you now? Our Matt has been exploring, with Christy Boy Columbus, young Gamey da Gama, and stout wee Cortez. And what did we discover, Matt, what realms of gold lay hidden among the bushes, in the ditch, and in the thorns?"

"Nothing, sir."

"Nothing, sir, nothing? Nothing will come of nothing, Matt, as the old unfortunately English bard would have it.

A nest, maybe, Matt? A nest?"

I could think of nothing to say. Wait. Get it over. Do not set up a nettle-field of lies, he'd lay me down, naked, within it. There was no way out. His fingers were thrumming on the desk, louder and louder. Thrumming.

"Did you rob a nest, Matt? Did you find a nest, answer me boy."

"No sir, I didn't touch it."

"Ha! so there is a nest, then, Matt? Is there a nest?"

"Yes, sir, a greenfinch's nest."

Not a word more did he say, but swept from the classroom, leaving us in a welter of whisperings. I looked round at Big Con Rohan. His fist clenched, he shook it at me. I looked away. I had not lied. I had not told the truth.

Master Brosnan came back, the little brown foetus in his hand. He put it down on the desk before me. It was still as a piece of meat, pathetic, small. I protested my innocence, but he probed and prodded, and I could see my innocence becoming guilt, my truth becoming lies; I could feel the brown rhythm of the ticking clock over the fireplace, the vermilion collapse of a sod of turf in the grate, the breathing of the boys in their desks around me.

"Matt," pronounced Master Brosnan, poor Master Brosnan, "your punishment is not for the young bird's death, though that in itself merits severest punishment, but for your wallowing in deceit, for your insistence on the lie, your brazening out of untruths. Have you anything to say to me, now, Matt, anything at all that will avert your punishment?"

The silence grew; I could sense Big Con Rohan's heart stop its pumping, I knew his fists were clenched on the end of his desk. That was my reward. I let him suffer for as long as I dared. Then I lifted my head, looked Master Brosnan straight in the eye and said,

"No, sir, I have nothing more to say. I have told you the

truth, sir, and that is all I can say."

The Master hesitated, watching me. He knew there was more to it than that. A great deal more. But he was in a corner, too. Poor Master Brosnan. He went to the cupboard where he kept the slates and chalks and copies. He chose a sally rod, flexible, whip-thin, whine-perfect, that would send fire coursing through the palm, up the arm and through the entire body. He turned towards me. I had my hand out already, trembling, marked with dirt from the grass. Poor Master Brosnan. Poor man. Poor dreamer.

I stalked Big Con Rohan with the first gun I ever owned. There was a great deal of talk in those days, about guns; about war, and killing. I set out to kill Big Con Rohan. I would be an assassin, powerful, prowling, hidden.

Behind bushes, along hedgerows, behind boulders near the field edges, the meadow boundaries, the erratics, I stalked him. My gun fired pellets gouged out of raw potatoes. The gun was forced into the hard flesh, the spring drawn back, and a pellet, a flesh-coloured, moist scud was ready to be fired. It was a game. And I enjoyed it.

I was brought up with guns. My father kept a gun, a Mauser, delightful heft to it, balancing in the lifted hand with the bone of the shoulder-blade, so that to fire it was almost as easy as the shrug of a shoulder.

"Hold it with both hands," he told me, "have the left hand hold the right hand steady. Be ready for the kick of it and lift the barrel quickly after you shoot, to dissipate the force of the kick. Left eye closed. Right eye narrowed. Aim."

He stood at my left shoulder, I could feel the warmth of the words on my ear, he put his arms about me, his right hand holding mine on the gun, his left holding my arm firm. I knew the steadiness of his body, the restraining wall of his life against mine.

"When you aim," he said, "you must become your target. Take it all in, caress it, be in love with it for just this moment, know its secrets, know where it will hurt most, know where it is most vulnerable, imagine its death-wound already delivered, where it is, the open sore, and then touch it, gently, like a mother will touch the bleeding wound of her child. That is the trigger touch, Matt, do not touch the trigger in anger, never in anger, or you will miss, pull the trigger with sympathy, with sorrow, above all with love."

We knocked bottles off the wall thirty yards from the back door. Together we did it. Picked the spot, and the bottle burst into pieces. I could touch it with my palm from thirty yards away, I was able to run my hand up the cool, green side, feel the fading of its outline before it shrank towards the neck, I could find its source, below the neck, and I kissed that spot with affection, with the knowledge God must have of each man's pain and striving. I fired.

"Well done, Matt!" he said, slapping me on the back. "Now come and I'll show you where I hide it. You must never tell anybody where it is; if the others don't know where it is nobody can force them to tell. The Tans could force anyone to tell, but they can't if they don't know. But you'll know. And I might need you to know. Some day."

He brought me into the house. We climbed the half-stairs into the space over the kitchen; there was room here for one bed, no more; a partition closed it off from the rafters and the kitchen, the roof sloped down over the bed. He removed a timber lathe from the rafters; it slipped out easily, he pressed open a little hinged door in the timber; it was hollow inside, the Mauser fitted snugly. I caught my breath at the perfection of the hide. He laughed and put the timber back. As he reached up to put it in its place I got the smell of his sweat, and it was a reassuring smell, comforting, a strong male smell of sheltering places. How I loved him then, and loved his trust in me, and I longed to be able to tell him what it meant to me, if only I had the words.

There was hope of war at that time, the great promise of violence. It was the lovely, jerky movement of history; and I was part of it then, part of a strange, twilight, history. A lorry was to pass along the Glenshale Road, coming from town, heading to the village barracks. The Volunteers knew that only eight men would be accompanying a load of rifles, ammunition, and a few boxes of gelignite, being delivered in stages from Dublin; this was the last leg of their journey. Most of the men in the townland, including my father, and Master Brosnan, were in on the event. Some of the children. Including me. Big Con Rohan, too, forgiving, and forgiven.

For days I saw them work out the details of the ambush. Each evening two men went out to the Glenshale Pass, digging trenches at the base of the hill. They had one of the children with them to keep watch. There was a point high up on Slievefad, the Eagle's Nest we called it, a ledge jutting out from an escarpment, and by lying down on it, your face out over the edge, you could see for at least a mile in each direction along the Glenshale Road.

I was watch for one of those evenings; it was exhilarating, and dull! My father and Master Brosnan were together inspecting the hollows dug out behind boulders on the hill side of the Pass, then they went across to the rhododendron wood to finish a fosse dug just in off the road. I was on the ledge. Lying on my belly. I could see the lake, the hill slopes, the road. I tried out the whistle: two quick blasts for danger, three longer, slow blasts for the all clear. My father waved up at me. They got to work.

I was in short trousers still, though I was in sixth class

in Drumdouglas school. I thought about getting long trousers after participating with the men in this event. Soon Ireland would be free; FREE! after centuries; and I was to be part of it.

The clacking of pick-axes, the slicing of spade and scraping of shovel, rose to me with surprising clarity. I was bored, shifting uncomfortably on my belly. I watched a kestrel hovering level with my eye; it was beautiful, almost motionless, lying on its invisible dish of air, then it veered sharply, diving close to earth. I lost its flight in the gathering dusk.

A light drizzle began to come in over the lake. I was hoping this might send us all home but the men kept digging, steadily, the occasional mumble of their voices reaching me. I was shivering with cold when I saw a faint light in the distance, coming from the direction of the town. For a long moment I was stupefied into immobility. Then I whistled, sharply, twice; I could just make out the shapes among the rocks down below; they vanished, instantly, like shadows, a night silence descending all at once.

I heard the noise of the engine. It grew steadily louder, roared once or twice in the changing of gears as it came up the slope, then steadied into an angry whine as it passed along the road beneath. I thought, from the high-pitched note of its engine, from its black shape outlined against the darkness of the bushes, from its headlights and their position in relation to the tail lights, that it must be a Crossley Tender. The enemy. Passing under the sharpened claws of the hawk. I heard raucous voices raised in laughter. They passed; the sounds began to fade, the tail-lights glowed a while, the sickly white headlights picking out the road, patches of hillside, fields. Then they were gone. There was a moment of silence. I whistled again, three times. I had come of age. I was involved. I was a "Volunteer."

In the late morning of the following Saturday, about twenty-five men converged on the Glenshale Pass. Only three of the boys were allowed to come; I was one, walking tall and proud beside my father. It was a beautiful, autumnal day; the lake reflected blue, there was no trace of clouds. The rhododendron bushes were absolutely still, the gorse bushes on the hill slope glowed with their saffron fire. We all converged on the Pass from different directions, trying not to attract notice, because there are eyes everywhere, in the bushes, behind the walls, and whisperings, and telephones. I was to be lookout on the town side; Manus Cafferky lookout at the other end and Jimmy Harte was to take up position in the middle of the Pass.

I felt old, proud, and scared. I waved to Manus and Jimmy and began my climb up the shale-strewn slope to the Eagle's Nest. I edged out onto the rock, creeping on my stomach, and looked out over the Pass. At the town end I could see three men already in position. Beneath me there were six, all in their dugouts, settling themselves, chatting quietly. I knew there were more men in the fosse across the road but I could not see them. I could just make out Manus at the far end of the Pass and under his position five more men.

Under Jimmy's ledge, about midway between me and Manus, were four men on either side of the road. There were three vehicles expected, the munitions lorry, a Crossley Tender in front of, and one behind, the lorry. The tenders were to be attacked first, together, putting the main body of guards out of action, destroying the vehicles, blocking any chance of escape for the lorry.

By midday the Glenshale Pass looked peaceful. How much of a lie the world can be! It was warm up on my ledge on Slievefad; I could just make out my father in his culvert below me and to the right; I could see Master

Brosnan with him. The tension I felt lifted before the seeming normality of the day, the men chatting easily, the lake across the road sparkling in the light. Suddenly there was a shout from Manus Cafferky. Something like a mushroom hardened deep inside my stomach.

It was about twenty minutes after twelve. The convoy had not been expected until one. Manus's shout was quickly followed by two shrill blasts from his whistle. The Tans were on their way. Almost at once I could hear the sounds of their engines, louder than normal across the still air. I huddled into the texture of my rock, my stomach tightened, my fingers clutching at the shingly soil. I could see the men draw their bodies deeper into their positions, rifles poised and ready. The sound of the engines was an obscenity in that place, at that time, their growl, their rumour, their threat. I could feel a harsh pounding in my ears; I found it hard to breathe; I was high above the road, and hidden. Terrified.

There was a long period of waiting as the noise of the engines grew. A heron was rising from the shore, flopping slowly and heavily out over the lake, then turning, languidly, effortfully, back towards the rhododendron bushes and the road. It was big, uncomely, its flapping regular and laboured. At the same time I could see the first Crossley coming round the bend under Manus's lookout place, at the far end of the Pass. The convoy straightened out onto the road, the lorry about twenty yards behind the tender, a second tender just coming into view some thirty yards back. The truck was covered in a heavy, grey, tarpaulin.

It was all so dreamlike, almost a slow game, and yet the engines were loud, the combined revving and gear-changing made the air throb; I imagined the shale on the hillside reverberating under the thrust and effort of the convoy, the air riven by the chaos and anger of the noise.

Again I saw the heron, its flight still low and steady; it had come out over the road, into view of the first tender. And then I saw an arm reach out from the tender; there was a loud report and the heron scrawked, rose slightly, then plunged in a whirl of neck and legs and body, ungainly, ugly, sad, onto the centre of the road. The tender carried on, and I imagined the laughter within. The second tender, unaware of what had happened, stopped; those inside had heard the sound of a shot and were taking no chances. The first tender and the truck reached the ambush points, the tender immediately under me, between two rows of men, the lorry further back but moving, inevitably, towards the trap.

There was a sudden, awful noise from the rifles, all the men below me aiming directly at the first tender. Almost at once the vehicle burst into flames and slewed across the road to smash hard into the stone wall. The truck was carried forward by its momentum until it, too, was between the ambush points. Sustained rifle fire was turned towards it, towards the wheels and cab. The second tender had begun to reverse at speed, quickly passing beyond the immediate aim of the ambushers under Manus's viewpoint. The soldiers got out and dived for the edge of the road, disappearing from my sight. There was confusion. Above the rifle shots I could hear shouts of command, occasional screams; I saw a soldier half fall, half run from the first, burning tender; his whole body was on fire, he staggered across the road towards the rhododendrons, hands raised hopelessly in the air; then he fell, face down, burning.

The engine of the truck had stopped. The four soldiers in the first tender were dead, their bodies inside the burning vehicle, apart from the man who had fallen out on the road. The other tender could be seen in the middle of the bend at the far end of the Pass, engine running, its occupants nowhere visible. There were shouts from Manus

Cafferky's father, and several men left their ambush places to surround the truck. Manus himself kept shouting about the positions of the soldiers from the third tender but it was difficult to hear what he was saying.

There was silence, then, as the men approached the covered truck. Master Brosnan called to the men he believed were in the back of the truck that they should surrender, promising them they would not be harmed.

"Step out, throw your guns onto the road, NOW!"

His words rose clearly through the bright, clean air, to where I lay; I thrilled at the familiar voice, at its authority, its pride, its strength. Again there was silence. Two rifles were flung out from the back of the truck and clattered onto the road. Two Tans followed, lifting the tarpaulin flaps, climbing down over the tailboard. They stepped back from the truck, hands held high. I knew their fear from the tense hold of their bodies, from the way they glanced around, anticipating bullets. I could hear the still running engine of the third tender and the crackle of the fire in the first one, down and to my left. Three Volunteers went cautiously to the cab of the truck and dragged out two bodies onto the road; then they climbed into the truck and the slamming shut of the cab doors resounded across the Glenshale Pass.

Two more Volunteers came around the truck and peered into the back; then they hammered hard on the side of the truck; it roared into life and began to move off, making its way round the burning tender, gathering speed until it turned the corner and headed away towards the village. The Tans were standing patiently on the road. Master Brosnan began to say something when there was a sudden storm of rifle shots; I saw the Master flung from the centre of the road into the rhododendron bushes. Two Volunteers fell where they were and the rest opened fire at once, killing the two Tans. It was carnage, horrible, sudden, overwhelming.

Sporadic firing went on for some time and I could see Manus gesticulating and pointing. I kept wondering if my father had been hit, I had not seen him rise from his place in the ambush. At last I heard the tender's engine rev up powerfully; the Auxiliaries had managed to get back into it and reversed it out of sight. It must have turned and raced, then, back the way it had come. The silence of the autumn afternoon settled back slowly on the Pass. One of the Tans jerked where he lay on the road, like a trout landed and forgotten on the bank, shivering into death. I realised I had been sweating, my clothes were damp, I was suddenly very cold. I remember reaching the back of my wrist across my forehead and watching the tiny streams of sweat that came away among the veins, how soiled the sweat was with dust.

The greatest fear of all is the fear that lurks in waiting, knowing with certainty that they will come, that they will come with ire, with a desire for revenge deep in their hearts, urging their bodies to desperate acts.

Two days passed, wet, dark days, and they did not come. On the afternoon of the third day, as we were sitting close to the fireplace, rain and wind wrapping us in a pleasurable cocoon, I had begun to let go of that fear. Mother was knitting; Thomas was fiddling with cards at the small table and Delia was standing on the other side of the hearth, poking at the fire lazily, her mind miles and miles away. The dinner was stewing in the oven; father was outside somewhere; he had gone out wrapped in his black rainclothes, his greattrousers, coat, wellingtons, even his black fisherman's hat. I heard nothing, nothing but wind and rain.

They simply booted the door open in front of them, crashing it back against the wall, and they were inside, bursting in with the rains and the storms, in through the smashed door, into the small, cosy kitchen of our lives.

There were five of them, three dressed in that dark green cloth that was almost black, their huge capes hanging down about them, but their hands and their guns out against us; they were the regular members of the Royal Irish Constabulary and they did not terrify me so much. The other two were not "Black and Tans", they were Auxiliaries, wearing the dark blue uniforms and dark green bonnets we had come to dread. These two also had great black capes hanging about their bodies, giving them the appearance of huge, night predators. They stood a moment, watching us, their capes hanging down about them, like canvas tents, the rain sluicing off them, as off un-chuted roofs, spilling onto the dry flags of our kitchen.

They had crowded in on top of us before we could take a breath, their bulk, their noise, their announced violence, filling the small room with a stifling terror. We had jumped up with the fright of it, all except my mother who sat, needles poised, as if solidified. One of the Tans was shouting, screaming orders at us; they had rifles raised and pointed but what I noticed at once was that each rifle had its bayonet fixed. I remember the sheen, the dark iron piece that clamped the blade to the barrel, the deep groove that ran along the blade, like a living vein, the exceptional brilliance of the edge, the slightly rounded point that could, with a sudden thrust, pass clean through coat, waistcoat, shirt and vest, puncture the flesh and travel deep into the bowels.

"Up! up! you fucking bitch you, up!" the Tan was shouting; slowly, then, very slowly, mother rose from her chair, holding her needles, raising her hands shoulder high.

"The man of the house, where is he?" the Tan shouted at my mother. I answered for her, feeling my responsibility as the oldest male, almost finished primary school, already

having a part in the great battle. I knew a terror that was
moving like a coldness through my body, but my mind was
perfectly clear, lucid, like a mountain stream.

"He's gone out to look after the cattle," I said, "up in
the hill field."

They paused, but only for a moment.

"Faces to the wall, all of you!" the Tan screamed at us,
gesturing with his bayonet towards the back wall of the
kitchen. I saw mother leave her knitting down slowly on
the chair, with infinite care, irritating the officer who
screamed an obscenity at her. She stopped and looked at
him; I was astonished at the grimace of complete contempt
that was obvious on her face. He screamed again at her.

"You filthy Irish whore! up against the wall or I'll rip
your ugly old body into shreds. Up! up! up!" darting his
bayonet at her, dangerously close. Slowly she turned and
faced the wall. She was on my left, Thomas on my right,
whimpering quietly with fright. Delia was on the other side
of Thomas, pale as water, stiffened with terror. One of the
Tans jerked our hands up so that we were forced to lean
forward against the wall, our hands high up in front of us.
Then he put his rifle down and began to run his hands
over us, my body first, searching. There was silence as his
hands patted and probed; as he reached into the inside
pocket of my jacket I could hear the hammering of the
rain, the anger of the wind, the running of water just
outside the smashed-open door; I could even hear the
crackling of the fire and the loud breathing of the enemy.

The soldier moved to my mother and ran his hands
over her body, too; she remained silent; I glanced towards
her, he was handling her roughly, feeling her breasts, her
waist, her thighs, down along her legs. She stared at the
wall without a change of expression though I knew how
livid with anger and humiliation she must have been. The
soldier grunted something, the others guffawed, then he

came to Thomas. Thomas was crying openly, his mouth blubbering silently, tears coming down his face, but he stood bravely, his head high, as the hands worked over him. Then it was Delia's turn. The Tan grunted in anticipation.

She was fourteen, a big girl, pretty, too; she had small, swelling breasts; she wore a long dress down to her ankles but the way she had to lean against the wall emphasised the potency of her body, the pushing of the breasts, the growing fullness of her buttocks. One of the soldiers said something; they all laughed and the Tan moved towards his task.

Slowly his hands travelled over her, touching her breasts, lingering over them. I could see the tension growing over Delia's face, the anguish gathering, the humiliation, the hatred. His hands moved downwards, lingering again about her waist, moving over her buttocks, pressing them, down along her thighs and calves to her bare feet. Then he stood back. I sighed with relief. Three of the Tans moved away about the house, they turned over chairs and tables, burst into the kitchen cupboard and scattered saucepans and crockery onto the floor where it clattered and smashed.

"Guns!" the first Tan shouted, "just tell us where they are and we'll leave you in peace."

I turned my head – "There are no guns here; we have nothing to do with … "

I noticed the Tan who had searched us. He was smirking roundly and had picked up his rifle again. He whispered to the sergeant who glanced quickly towards Delia.

"Face the wall, you lying Irish bastard!" he screamed at me and I turned back quickly. One of the Tans had gone into the lower bedroom and I could hear him breaking things apart down there. Another went out the back door into the yard. The third climbed the steps to the settle room. My mind followed him up there; I began to pray.

I could see, out of the side of my eye, the Tan moving his rifle with its fixed bayonet towards Delia's back. He lowered the bayonet to the floor and began to raise the hem of Delia's dress with it, higher, higher. I could hear Delia begin to sob. I knew she was wearing nothing under her dress. I saw her body stiffen, I heard the heavy breathing of the Tan, the smashing and crashing of things all about us. Delia's dress rose higher and higher. Up over her white, delicate calves, past the frail-looking, innocent, hocks of her knees, up the firm, beautiful thighs. I turned and shouted at him.

"You leave my sister alone! You have no right to behave like that. Stop it or I swear I'll kill you... !"

He looked at me, astonished.

"You get the hell out of this house now! all of you!" I continued. I clenched both my fists and stepped towards him. The sergeant laughed out loud. The Tan took his bayonet away from Delia's dress and turned it towards me. I heard Mother call out softly, pleadingly, "Matt! Matt!" but I did not care. A great fury had risen within me and I had to do something. I advanced towards the Tan, my right fist drawn back, ready.

He raised the rifle towards me; the point of the bayonet touched my chest; the leer on his face had changed to an expression of amazement and hesitation; for the moment I had the initiative and I knew he was more unsure of himself than I was. I was twelve years of age; but I was big now, and strong, and in a fury. He watched me; I glared into his eyes; I saw Delia's body ease back into relief even while she turned her face anxiously towards me. And then there was the sound of a shot, just outside the back door. Almost at once another, loud and startling, seeming to drown out, by the noise and suddenness, the sounds of smashing furniture, of wind and rain.

For a moment both soldiers still in the kitchen looked away from us towards the door; I jumped forward and pushed aside the young Tan's bayonet, placing myself between him and Delia. His face grew ugly with anger; very deliberately he turned the rifle back towards me and I was certain I was going to die. My God! but I stood proud and unafraid in front of Delia; I was strong, and in command. I knew I had won; it would be only the violence of the gun that could defeat me. The forced, ultimately meaningless weight of the rifle pitched against my truth. The Tan's lips parted and I could see him clench his teeth to shoot. But the sergeant shouted at him to come with him to the door. The others had come from the rooms, and were taking up positions round the door, their guns aimed towards it as if they expected an attack.

"Leave, them, Jim!" the sergeant said, "leave the kid! He's OK, Jim, he's plucky. Leave him, for the moment anyway. Let's see what the friggin' hell is goin' on outside!"

There were three more shots from the yard. Then, just as the sergeant was about to kick out the door we heard a whoop of glee from outside. The sergeant hesitated, then lifted the latch and pushed open the door. The Tan who had gone out into the yard stood at the open half-door to one of our sheds. We all crowded forward after the Tans to see, Delia squeezing my arm gratefully, my mother, too, gripping me by the waist and shaking me, soundlessly. Thomas was still crying in his fear, rubbing his face, ashamed, with the backs of his hands. I took him by the shoulder and gave him a strong hug; he looked up at me and smiled, he sobbed and nodded his head.

"The hens, sarge," the soldier shouted, "the bleedin' hens gave me the fright of my life. Flapped out at me from nowhere. Thought they were friggin' Irish bastards!"

Along the wooden rails inside the shed we could see

several hens, dead. Another emerged from the shed just then and scampered, clucking wildly, along the concrete shore of the yard. The young soldier who had teased Delia raised his rifle quickly and shot. The hen gave a sudden awful squawk and rose into the air in a small explosion of feathers, then tumbled wing over head over claw, into an ungainly dying; it jerked in quick spasms for a few moments, and lay still. The Tan grinned. The others laughed. The rain came down heavily; it was a scene of stupidity and shame and I reacted again, foolishly perhaps, out of a sense of anger and frustration.

"Well done!" I said, quietly, "very well done indeed!"

This time the young bully did not hesitate; he swung the back of his wrist into the side of my head; I was knocked backwards against the jamb of the door; I was stunned and sat down heavily on the wet ground.

The sergeant had been stung into some sort of shame by my words and the sight of the carnage in the yard.

"Enough!" he shouted, "let's get the hell out of this dump!"

He turned and pushed past my mother, past Delia and Thomas, back into the kitchen. The others followed; they tramped heavily through the kitchen, kicking at any furniture still intact as they went by. The young bully waited until last then, as he passed me, he hammered the butt of his rifle hard into the right-hand side of my chest. I felt, then, as if he had smashed my body open; my breath exploded out of me, a terrible pain, like fire, took hold of my entire body; I coughed for breath, I fell backwards onto the cement floor of the yard. Then I fainted.

When I surfaced I was on my knees in the yard, doubled over, getting violently sick. Mother was on her knees, too, on the rain-soaked ground, holding me, her hand soothing my brow, whispering to me as the spasms took me, holding me, holding me, ...

"Darling" she was saying, "hush, darling, hush my lovely boy, so good, so brave, so strong, so foolish ... hush, hush, hush now," as to a baby clamped sobbing to her breast.

But a fine happiness glowed within me, through the pain, through the rain that came blanketing down, through the sickness, the anger, the hurt. It was a moment of pride and tenderness I have never forgotten. Her gentle hand on my forehead, soothing, that firm grip around my shoulders, my sister Delia, too, on the other side of me, on her knees, a towel in her hand with which she wiped my face, to cleanse me, and all of us, from what that day had brought. There was in me a sense of belonging that could not ever be denied me, a flowering of passion through the filth and stupidity of the time. For a while then I thought I might die; I felt it would be a great way to go, locked up in extremes of tenderness, duty done, care for those I loved made manifest, my vision clear, my place in their hearts secure.

They brought me inside when my body had quietened and they set me cosily beside the fire. Delia and Thomas began to straighten up the furnishings and clear out the broken delft. Mother put on a great black kettle of water to boil over the fire; she went down into the bedroom for fresh clothes and towels and when she came back she was pale at the wanton destruction she had seen.

"They broke the mirror of the dressing-table," she said as she was helping me out of my jacket and shirt, "they tore open the wardrobe, smashed the tallboy and pulled every little thing out of every drawer, they buried their bayonets in the bed, through eiderdown and blankets and sheets, into the mattress itself, ripping everything before them."

She poured the boiling water into a basin and emptied cold water in from the bucket, making sure it was all just so; then she dipped in a towel and rubbed me gently all over my face and chest and back, dipping, rubbing, squeezing it out as if she were exorcising all that evil between her hands; several times she emptied and refilled the basin, cleansing me, washing my head, my hair, my ears, my neck, washing most gently of all the great purple hurt in my mind, touching with lovely kindness the inflamed map of a rifle butt high on my chest. My breathing came easier, the sharpness of the pain eased to a dull throbbing ache, and as she washed my feet in the lovely, hot water, I laid my head back against the top of the chair and floated into sleep.

DAVID

WAS IT ONLY WEDNESDAY THAT HE SAID TO ME, BLOOD DRIPPING slowly into his arm, death a face already leering in at him from beyond the window:

"So many of them, out there dying in the Gulf, young, healthy men, hardy, hopeful, and their deaths so horrible and unnecessary, their lives squandered by the hypocrites who want power for themselves. Terrible, a terrible war. So many of them will die, horribly. You'd wonder why they bother to keep the likes of me alive."

He gestured towards the tube inserted in his arm, there were tears in his eyes, he shook his head, like a proud horse, shaking off the thought, as if, already, he had begun to block out our world, to get deep down inside himself, to wrestle his spirit into submission for death.

Father.

"It'll be a good day to die," he said, and I had nowhere to turn, I had nothing left to hold on to, I had no words to offer.

A good day to die!

MATTHEW

WHEN I WOKE AGAIN IT WAS A PLEASANT SPRING EVENING. THEY had set the kitchen to rights while I slept; they had dressed me in a football shirt that was warm and clean. They had stood the door up against the jamb, leaving gaps through which I could see the evening. I fancied I could see steam rising from the flagstones of the front path.

My first thought was for the room over the kitchen. I knew they had not found the gun but they might have done sufficient damage to the room to disturb it and, if they should come back again – and they often did that hoping to catch people off their guard – they might find it. I moved cautiously, trying to stand up. I was stiff and sore about the chest, I felt weak but I could move about well enough. Mother tried to make me stay quiet but I climbed the steps into the room. They had shattered everything, the bed had been ripped to pieces, the bedclothes torn to shreds. But the hidingplace had not been touched – not a sign, not a breath, not a blink.

I heard someone come rushing into the kitchen below. For a moment I imagined it was the Tans returning. I looked down; it was Manus Cafferky, and he stood stricken into stupor by the destruction all around him.

"My God!" he murmured, "they've surely given you a visit. Where's Matt?" He shouted the last two words, flinging them abruptly against my mother.

"I'm up here!" I called to him, and the effort caused a quick jab of pain to shoot across my chest.

"It's your father, Matt," he called up to me, "you're to get the gun and all the ammunition and you're to come at once to our house. Your father's there, with my father and Michael Tierney. The Tans are below, moving up the Hill Road, searching all the farms. Our house is the last one on the road, up on the hill and father can't move; they shot him in the leg out on the Glenshale Pass; his leg is near shattered. It's in plasters and everything and he can't be shifted. If the Tans find him they'll know for sure. We'll all be shot."

I had already lifted off the board and taken down the gun and the little boxes of ammunition. I came down the steps carefully. So. It wasn't over yet. Manus was going on, half talking, half whispering, gesticulating.

"There's about twenty of them; they've shot Peter Earley, they found the rifle he had hidden under the cart in the shed. They just put him up against the gable wall of his own house and they shot him. And they shot James Ryan, and Mrs Ryan, they took husband and wife out onto the road and they told them to run, run like Hell, they said, and maybe we won't shoot you, and they ran, the pair of them, shouting and screaming, and some of the soldiers went down on their knees and they fired and fired and poor James and Annie were torn to bits by the bullets. Shot in the back they were, oh the dirty Tans, the cowards, do you know what they did then? went back into the house and into the room upstairs where old Seamus lay in bed. He hasn't left that bed for years the poor man, half deaf, half doting, and he asked the soldiers what was going on and they shot him, there, lying in his own bed would you believe that? The poor old bugger."

Manus sat down heavily on the couch, breathless, tears of anger widening his eyes. He jumped up again at once, shouted: "But we have to go, now, straight away!"

Mother noticed the gun in my hand and she gave a leap

of fright. She said nothing for a while. Then she took Manus by both shoulders and spoke slowly, very slowly.

"Manus, tell us exactly where Dan is, exactly what the message is, exactly how Matt is to get there, and what are the men plannin' to do!"

He looked back into her face. I could see him pulling his scattered thoughts together. He waited. Then he looked quickly at me and addressed his words to me.

"Mister Blake is above in my father's house. Michael Tierney is above with them. Tierney has a gun, but very little ammunition. Father is on a chair near the window, his leg up on an armchair; he has a rifle and a few bullets. Mister Blake wants to help fight off the Tans if they come as far as our house. Or at least make them think there's more people in it. Keep them at bay and hope that help comes. Matt is to take his bike and head in towards the village. After McGlynn's pub he's to take the hill road as far as Cash's old farm. On the way he's to tell the men at McGlynn's. Then he's to run over by the back of Hawthorn Hill, up our fields and into the yard of the house. He's to knock five times on the back door, making sure the Tans aren't there yet. He's to give the gun to Mister Blake and then go home the way he came. That's all Mrs Blake. And he's to go like the wind!"

Mother stood back from him, satisfied.

"So!" she said, not unkindly, looking at me, "there's conspiracy in my own home, behind my back is there? Now there's to be more heroics for you, lad. Are you up to it?"

"Yes, Mother," I said, my mettle high, "I surely am, rearin' to go!"

She watched me, she was thinking, thinking ...

"You'll take the bike, then," she said, "but you'll be mighty obvious to man and beast with that gun. And they might stop you and search you. There'll be Tans everywhere. I'll bet they're blocking the village on each side. How are you going to get through?"

We were silent. I couldn't think straight. Mother had to do the thinking, now. I waited. Trusting her.

"For Jesus sake, Mrs Blake," Manus begged, "for Jesus sake hurry up!"

Mother looked me up and down, her face brightening, her eyes beginning to sparkle.

"Is the leather football in the house?" she asked.

"Oh for Jesus sake, Mrs Blake," Manus wailed.

I opened the cupboard under the stairs and took out the ball. It was a large old ball, of polished leather, sewn, containing a rubber bladder that had to be pumped up. It was laced tight.

"Quickly now," she said, "unlace it, let all the air out."

I undid the laces and released the long neck of the bladder and untied it – the air came out with a great sigh. I squeezed the ball, flattening it. She took it from me, took the gun and the little boxes of bullets and pushed them inside the ball. Then she told me to pump up the bladder again and to lace the whole thing together. I did; I rounded the ball as well as I could; it was not perfect, bulges here and there; but – it might do!

"You already have your football jersey on," she said; "go now, and may God be with you! Hang your boots from one of the handlebars, the ball from the other. Go, son, go!"

I went out into the yard. The undergrowth smelt fresh after the rain, the world exhaling, stretching itself towards the peace of evening. I hoped the visibility of the ball hanging from the handlebars would conceal it from any searching gaze. The bike was my father's, big, high, a dark desert camel. As I threw my leg over the saddle I gasped with the pain in my chest. Mother stood at the door. I grinned at her. Then I was off down the lane towards the road.

The road led downhill almost all the way to the village. It was easy going, pleasant even, apart from the ache in my chest and a pounding fear in my heart. The ball swung innocently, the boots were tied tightly around the other side; my red football jersey must have flashed among the foliage along the sides of the road. I pedalled hard; the road was gritty; I was in a race, I was going to have to win.

And then, inevitably, around a corner I saw the tender drawn across the road. There were at least ten soldiers standing around it. Now, if one or more of the five who had been in our house were among this lot ...

I skidded to a halt before the tender. One of the Tans came towards me – the others merely glanced and went on chatting and smoking.

"A match on, then?" he asked. I nodded.

"Who's playing?"

"Drumdouglas and Glenamass," I answered quickly. "I'm with Drumdouglas. Midfield."

He was walking slowly around me and the bike. There was a large black bag permanently fixed behind the saddle; I had forgotten about it. He opened it. He found a puncture repair kit, nothing more.

"Right!" he said, and slapped me sharply on the back. "Off you go now, and good luck to Drumdouglas! Remember: if you can't get the ball, get the man!"

His slap almost killed me; the pain was atrocious, and my breath seemed to vanish with the spasm it caused me. I gasped. He laughed.

"You'll need to be a mite fitter than that, young lad, I'd say," and then he reached for the ball. When he touched it, it swung gently away from him. I wheezed and gasped, exaggerating to distract his attention. "A bit soft, your ball, I'd say," he offered. "You'd want to pump it up for the game."

"One of the Glenamass lads has a pump," I managed to

say, but he had already turned away, forgetting me; he went back to his comrades, chuckling to himself. I mounted quickly, and was gone.

I took great, heaving breaths to ease the pain. I came to McGlynn's pub in a few minutes. There were three men standing in the evening sun, leaning against the gable wall, each holding a pint of porter. They looked indolent and at ease, but they were deep in earnest conversation. I recognised one of them as Patsy Gillis, one of the men who had been out on the Glenshale Pass. As I slewed the bike across the gravel in front of them he called out to me. I told him of father's plight in Cafferky's house on the hill. I told him, too, of the tender five minutes out along the road. He took a great drink out of his pint, wiped his mouth with his sleeve, threw back his shoulders.

"Off you go, carefully now, Mattie Blake. We'll see if we can't arrange a little excitement for these buckos!"

As I began to push the bike up the rough stone laneway that led by the pub's gable, Patsy Gillis was heading back into the pub with the other men. Soon I had to leave the bike against a ditch and make the rest of the distance on foot. I untied the ball and crossed into a meadow. The wind blew little waves across the grasses; somewhere off to my left I could hear the *nyaek-nyaek* of a corncrake. I kept to the edge of the meadow, following the ditches. I climbed over the heathery part of the hill and came to Cafferky's back fields. At last I was climbing over the wooden gate that led into the yard. Everything was peaceful; their old dog Rex lay in a corner of sunshine near the rain-barrel. His tail wagged gently when he saw me. There was a scatter of turf-sods up against a wall, a dark-mould patch of earth forming a map of where the clamp had been.

I paused, straddling the top bar of the gate, gazing onto Cafferky's yard, at the back of the long, low house, its whitewashed walls, its perfect thatch, the small windows with bright-blue paint; beyond were a few straggling mountain ash and one great oak; behind me were fields and the hill and the wide stretch of countryside I knew so well. This was my place, my kingdom, traced out, tracked through; for the first time ever I knew I loved that place, everything about it, I love it still, perhaps you get to love something all the more as soon as it seems you may lose it, it catches you in the throat, lifts your spirits with pride then urges a great sob of loss into your chest.

I dropped gently into the yard and rapped as I'd been instructed on the back door. Almost at once the latch was lifted and Father's face lit up with relief when he saw me. Eagerly I began to tell him of the day's adventures but he hushed me at once. "Later, later, Matt," he said. He took the ball from me and quickly undid the laces, took out the gun and bullets and smiled grimly.

"Well done, Matt," he said, quietly, and I blushed at the pride I could see in his eyes. "Go now, lad, go back home. Keep the door closed tight till my getting back to you. Mind your mother, Matt, and Delia, and Thomas. Mind them. Tell them I'll see them soon. Quick now, lad, go, go, go!"

Before I could say anything further to him he was turning from me, back into the house. As the old, blue door began to close on him I had the feeling I would never see him alive again. That this would be my last image of him, turning from me into the dimness of Cafferky's house, the gun in his hands, his face intent, war surrounding him. There was a great deal I wanted to say; I knew I would not find the words for it but if I could even touch him – so that he'd know …

"Dad!" I called to him, impulsively, he stopped, and I could see he knew what it was I wanted to say.

I hesitated. Then, "You know I love you, Dad?" I

stammered, embarrassed, glad to have it out.

He put his hand gently on my shoulder and smiled.

"Of course, Matt, of course I know that. But now I want you to go home. You'll be needed there. God be with you now, Matt."

It was enough. I smiled at him, then I was hurrying back across the yard towards the barred gate.

I have often wondered what would have happened had that soldier found the gun in my football. Perhaps, with the speed and vituperation with which things were being done at that time, I might have been shot, or hung. I would have held my head high, walking to their gallows, or standing upright before their firing squad. I would have been a hero; I would have become fabulous, a name to be murmured with awe throughout the whole of Ireland for ever! How simple that would have been, pointed, heroic, a life and death accomplished with dignity, clean edges, direction! I climbed back over Cafferky's old gate.

I circled round the high fuchsia hedge by the Cafferky house and came to the clump of ash trees to the west of their small front garden. Everything was so still and peaceful it was difficult to believe the air was blue with terror. I climbed into one of the trees, in amongst the leaves. I climbed until I could see parts of the laneway leading up to the house from the Ryan farm. I could see smoke rising from the burning of the Earley house. I would brave anything to prevent the Tans reaching Cafferky's, finding Father there.

I waited; the slender leaves of the ash whispered and brushed softly together; the top of the tree where I was hiding swayed gently, more with my weight than with any breeze. I imagined myself sitting in a small boat on a lake, the almost motionless waters lulling me into dreaminess; I was a gliding swan, a harrier surveying his territory, a branch of the ash, part of the landscape, a leaf, a feather, birdsong.

From out of that landscape a poem came to my mind that Master Brosnan had taught us, so often chanted as he moved in a trance around the classroom, held by the rhythms and sounds so that we felt no embarrassment before him, no self-consciousness in the emotions the poem roused in us:

Oh the Erne shall run red
With redundance of blood,
The earth shall rock beneath our tread,
And flames wrap hill and wood,
And gun-peal, and slogan cry
Wake many a glen serene,
Ere you shall fade, ere you shall die,
My Dark Rosaleen!
My own Rosaleen!
The Judgement Hour must first be nigh,
Ere you can fade, ere you can die,
My Dark Rosaleen!

As if I were coming slowly out of a dream I realised I was looking at five soldiers moving up the road from Ryan's house. They were still a quarter of a mile away, moving cautiously, in single file close to the whitethorn hedge, rifles ready, their capes threatening in the lovely evening.

I climbed down from the tree, to warn my father they were on the way. I feared his quick anger that I had not obeyed him yet I knew it was essential they be prepared. I climbed, trying not to stir a leaf on my ash tree; my heart thumped so wildly I was convinced the Tans on the road below might hear it.

All at once there was an explosion down in the valley. It echoed through the hill and faded away into the evening and then I could hear the sounds of rifle fire. I climbed back up the tree from where I could see a cloud of smoke rising down near the main road. I watched the Tans on the lane hesitate, consult with one another and then, to my relief, turn and move quickly back down the way they had come. I guessed that Patsy Gillis had gathered a few of the men and attacked the soldiers on the road. Quickly now I came down from the tree and ran round the back of the house. I knocked and Father opened; I told him of my meeting with Patsy, what I had seen on the lane. Then we sat in silence inside the house as the evening darkened; soon the sounds of shooting, too, began to die away.

After a short time I told Father I would go cautiously down the lane; there was no point in us all waiting in fear when the Tans had probably long gone. He nodded to me and I was out the front door like a hare. It was dark on the laneway, hawthorn hedges rising high on either hand, the lane, sandy and brown, not yielding any light. I walked as quickly as I dared until suddenly I thought I glimpsed figures ahead of me; they vanished almost as soon as I had seen them and I began to wonder if my imagination was teasing me again. Everything was still; above my head, in that dim space of sky between the tops of the bushes, I could see the rapid, eerie flight of bats; I walked more slowly, glancing back to the small glow from the Cafferky window for reassurance. Suddenly the beam of a torch leaped full into my face and I cried out with the suddenness of it. There was a mumble of voices and figures broke from the shadows of the bushes all around me. I heard the voice of Manus Cafferky call my name; he ran to greet me and we hugged one another in relief.

Two

DAVID

The man was standing, up to his thighs in slip-water,
spinning; concentrated, eager, his hands
exact with rod and water-coloured gut;

I was digging in sand behind him, safe
from the wildering rush of the current;
periwinkles breathed small bubbles in the pools

and barnacles clung to the rough rock surfaces;
I hammered on their backs with stones
and watched the water-blood

seep from the shattered shells;
sometimes the shoals of mackerel broke
into the shallows near him, famished,

frenzied through the living mercury of eels;
I pictured them, out there, the shoals,
streaming through the cold, inhuman forests

of the underworld, aghast, and wraithlike;
the man was making his way homewards over rocks,
mackerel strung by their gills on twine,

fish-scales, fish-blood, ghosting his clothes
and I beside him, quietened,
clinging to his rough, red hands, for hold.

MATTHEW

MY BELOVED RUDGE! THE HEIGHT OF IT, ITS WEIGHT: NO GEARS TO ease it up the hills to Drommasheelin. To St Joseph's secondary school, the Christian Brothers. I had to get off and heave it up alongside me. My burden. Coming home was a different song! when the bike's weight and height carried me along, the impetus from each downhill glide floating me onwards. But, day after day, it was difficult, against winds, through rains, day after day, eight miles every morning, eight miles every afternoon.

One morning, early in the term, our history teacher, Brother Henry came in, told us to put away our books, sit back in our desks, listen, and wonder. As he walked up and down between the rows of desks, his hands gesticulating, he told us of Terence Mac Swiney. Just an ordinary man, he said, a dull man, an accountant even, imagine! profit and loss! desks, dust, pencils and rubbers; and yet – a man filled with the love of his people, with the love of his country. They made him Lord Mayor, he told us, because he was a man of the people, loved by the people, and he was arrested by the invader and thrown in gaol!

"He's at the mercy of the enemy, boys, and you know what that means! You all have experience of the way the English behave. They have torn our country into little pieces and tried to scatter the pieces to the winds. But Terence Mac Swiney is fighting back! he's fighting for God and country, boys, and I want you and me to fight with him, to send our message from this very classroom to the God of our Fathers that Terence Mac Swiney may prevail!"

He explained what a hunger strike was, how the Mayor refused all food the enemy offered him, how he had eaten nothing, not one crumb boys! not one drop of milk or one oatflake for sixty-four days! imagine that, boys, can you imagine it? sixty-four days! The weakness, the pain, the fearful gnawing of hunger at the innards, like a rat inside you, day after day, night after night, gnawing, gnawing, gnawing, and the whole world has turned its eyes on the little prison cell and is watching and listening and paying attention after all these centuries to the plight of the Irish people.

Brother Henry asked us to send, through God, a message of solidarity over the hills and valleys, across the sea, to the great Lord Mayor. As long as he was suffering we should suffer, too, small pangs of hunger compared to his, but we should do it. Would we hand up to him, of our own free will, mind! no forcing, no coercion – if you don't want to, boys, or if you feel yourselves not strong enough for the sacrifice, there will be no recriminations – hand up our lunches every day, our sandwiches, our milk, and he would take them all to the tinker camp on Cromlech Hill, and God would heed our sacrifices and Mary His Holy Mother would give Terence Mac Swiney the strength and we would win, boys! together, one great nation, we would win!

Eagerly we handed up our lunches, our bottles stoppered with brown paper, our thick slices of homemade bread softened with homemade jams, solemnly we laid them on Brother Henry's desk, holding his smile in our hearts, walking proudly to the tap outside, cupping our hands and drinking the mountain water. And every day Brother Henry wrote on the blackboard the number of days Mac Swiney had fasted.

"History, boys, history! History is not a list of dates and wars and battles copied out of a fat book into your skinny little copies. History is where you live, history is the air you breathe, history is your father and your mother, your brother and sister, it lives and grows up every lane in your townland, invades your homes, steals from you your daily bread. History is a great ocean and you are standing on its shores; there is a mighty wave swelling and breaking about your young, dry, bodies. Stand fast, boys, and the wave will leave you stronger than ever before, rich with the salt of the great ocean, your feet firmly planted on the earth, your hearts pounding with pride!"

The days passed. Sixty-eight. Sixty-nine. Seventy! That day was a particularly silent day for us; we went around stricken with awe. Even Brother Henry seemed restrained by the ongoing struggle. Seventy-one. Seventy-two. On the afternoon of that day I cycled home with Manus Cafferky.

About half-way home he called to me to follow him and we cycled off the road onto a cart-track. He stopped beside a turf-stack and threw down his bike. I followed. He winked at me, looked around carefully, then removed one of the sods on the side facing away from the road. He had stowed away four apples, two oranges, and a well-wrapped slice of blackberry pie! I was ravenous. We sat, our backs against the clamp, and shared the treasure. I was uneasy at this betrayal but that blackberry pie was good.

Seventy-three. Seventy-four. When we were told of Terence Mac Swiney's death, most of us cried. Brother Henry came into class and congratulated us on our great work. Then, to my dismay, he went round the whole class and shook hands with each of us, one after the other, holding the hand for a long moment, saying each boy's name. As he held mine I could feel the firmness of his clasp; when he spoke my name I lowered my eyes and hated myself, and hated Manus for leading me into the way of flesh. Brother Henry passed on, my hand tingled and I had to close my fist and rub my fingers along my trousers; I was a traitor, a failure, a coward. We stood as Brother Henry did the round; as he passed up another row he shook hands with Manus. Manus looked over at me, grinned, and winked. I felt worse than ever because my treachery was known to another. School was dismissed for the day. How a handshake can disturb you and the consciousness of treachery can settle like an ache on your palm so that you rub and rub, unable to ease the guilt that shifts, like a worm, under the skin.

We had only one terror, then, among the Brothers, Brother Canice. He taught us Irish, quickly destroying our natural instincts for the language through an excess of doctrinaire, grammatical constraints. If every little thing was not done to his liking trouble came upon us, trouble in a series of punishments. A simple mis-spelling was greeted with knocks on the knuckles from the hard wooden back of a duster; you closed your fist, palm upwards, exposing four ridges of fingers that end in the cliffs of your knuckles and – whap! down came the duster, glancing off the knuckles or landing square on the fingers. Ouch! the memory of it hurts, the hard clack of wood against knuckle-bone.

Canice was small, thin as barbed wire, grey-haired, his face pinched, sharp as a razor. When he handed out the punishment his lip lifted in a snarl, showing his teeth, gapped and ugly. If he heard a word of English in his class he took delight in writing the name into his notebook, along with the number of English words, and when the number reached a certain amount, the worst punishment was ordained: ten strokes with a sally rod on the bare arse!

Stephen Connors came to our school, a tinker boy from the camp beyond the crossroads. We gave him the loan of books, pencils and copies, we helped him catch up on the subjects. In return he brought us gifts, a tin mug, a horseshoe, strange painted miniatures. He spoke Irish beautifully, with a metallic twang in his voice that sounded like singing. He volunteered answers to Canice's questions, his hand shooting into the air, his red hair shaking with eagerness, his accuracy thwarting Canice's efforts to catch him out.

Then Martin Tubridy reached the awful tally of English words, blurted out the fatal "sandwich" during some quizzing he was getting, Canice standing before him, striking repeatedly at the boy's face. The brother dived at once for his notebook and his face lit up with delight as he announced the terrible number. Tubridy, his cheeks reddened from the slapping, was crying before Canice took out the rod, flexed it, swung it through the air several times.

I noticed Stephen Connors gripping the sides of his desk in horror; his whole body trembled with anger at the humiliation Tubridy had already been going through; now that flecked face was knotted in concentration, the lips clamped tight. I caught his eye; I shook my head slightly in warning. He looked away from me.

Canice motioned Tubridy to step up to the teacher's desk. The boy's face was melting butter, every muscle twitched, his nose was running, his mouth hanging open foolishly. We knew the routine. Tubridy took off his jacket and left it on the master's desk. Then he took off his pullover and laid that over the jacket. Next he pulled the braces down off his shoulders, and began, his hands almost uncontrollable, to undo the buttons on the fly of his trousers.

Stephen Connors's desk shook loudly and we heard his muffled cry, "No!"

Canice pounced on him, grabbed the diminutive tinker boy out of his desk and hauled him in front of the class.

He told him to stand without moving, he would deal with him as soon as he had finished with Tubridy. Connors gazed unflinchingly into Canice's eyes; I could see the tinker boy's hands had stopped trembling, I could see the fists knotted and ready, I knew he had made his decisions.

Canice turned back to Tubridy who stood, hoping for reprieve. Now his blubbering grew all the louder; he lowered his trousers round his ankles and hobbled like a maimed goat to the master's desk, bending over it, laying his sobbing face down into his pullover, gripping the sides of the desk with both hands. His soft, white buttocks were exposed and vulnerable, and Canice's eyes were wide with joy.

"Haagh!" he breathed aloud, flexing the rod once more between his hands, and advanced slowly to take up his position behind Tubridy and a little to the side. He settled his shoulders; he laid the rod across Tubridy's buttocks; we could see the flesh twitch and recoil at the touch. Canice raised his arm till it reached high behind his shoulders and then he brought it slicing down into Tubridy's quivering flesh. The boy screamed with the agony of it. We winced at the horror of the sound.

Without warning, Stephen Connors stepped forward and snatched the rod from Canice's hand. He broke it, slowly and deliberately, across his knee and flung the pieces against the classroom wall. Canice turned quickly towards him, grabbed him by the shoulders. Then Connors punched him, a sharp, vicious jab against his chin and the Brother's head jerked backwards, his face white with astonishment. Connors punched again, and again, the speed and accuracy of the blows compensating for the slightness of power behind them. Four, five blows landed on the old man's jaw; his back came up against the classroom wall; one more quick jab and the Brother's head had slammed back on the wall; he folded up and with extraordinary silence slid down the wall and crumpled up on the wooden floor. He lay there, moaning, at the feet of the red-haired tinker boy.

Connors turned and grinned at us.

"Good luck, lads!" he called out. "I wanted to do that from the moment I saw that bastard. Good luck to ye all! Ye've been good to me!"

Tubridy had forgotten his pain and moved like a robot, dressing himself again. Connors took Canice's wicked little notebook and put it in his pocket. "For the camp fire!" he laughed. Then he walked proudly down the classroom and out the door. Only then did I break loose from my astonishment; I began to clap my hands together in delight. At once the whole class joined me. We applauded, and cheered. Connors came back in for a moment and stood in the doorway, grinning at us, waving his hands over his head like a boxer. Then he was gone.

We never saw or heard of Brother Canice after that. I admired and even liked most of the other Brothers. The Bull Reagen used to use a sally rod, too, until after the news of young Connors got about. Soon after that The Bull drew a long strap of thick leather from his bag, all stitched into shape for him, he told us, by Sean the Shoemaker. When he used the leather it left the hands reddened and sore, but uncut, and the stinging died away much more quickly than the sting the sally rod had left.

DAVID

WE DROVE THE OLD FORD PREFECT BACK TO THE HEADLAND, parked it near the pier, and walked along the low cliff path to our preferred spot. How he strode then, waders folded down about his knees, I following after, running, stopping to fling a stone into the sea. It was a peaceful evening, the warmth of the day still clinging to the earth, the sun low on the horizon. A stonechat perched on a rock to watch us, and in the distance, somewhere in the mesh of small fields, a corncrake had begun its night drill, *nyaek-nyaek, nyaek-nyaek*, the harshness of its sound softened by distance into a soothing, rhythmic vesper.

We came down the cliff slope to a sheltered bay where there was a thin strip of beach. Here it was possible to catch a sea trout, or a salmon bass; and always there were pollack, heavier and darker in the deep water off the cliffs, lighter and more tasty among the smaller rocks near shore. And if you could spin out far enough there would be mackerel, shoals of them, passing close to us in the movement of the currents and of the tide.

He set up two rods, gave me a fine, silver-painted bait that trailed three deadly hooks out of its deceitful beauty, fitted it, with a weight, to the line, and let me start. He moved further, out onto the rocks, more skilful than I, able to draw his line in from the mouth of the bay, through the rocks, and back to shore. We fished. I did not care if I caught anything or not. I was happy. To be with him. There.

The shoals of mackerel passed, in the frenzy of their hunger bursting right onto the lip of the beach after the violently fleeing sprat. I caught one by sticking my foot in the water and kicking it up onto the sand. We landed several; I relished the pulse and throb out at the end of the line that sent a pleasurable excitement up the arm, into the rest of the body. But I could not kill them, could not take them off the hook and snap their heads back, as he could do. He laughed at me, indulgently, and killed them, clunck! suddenly, brown blood left on his fingers, and scales.

Once he caught a pollack, a big one that felt, he said, as if he were hauling in a stone, no fun to it, no thrill, only deadness. It was too big for him to put his thumb in behind the gills and snap back the head, so he lifted it high above his shoulders and slapped it on a rock. Several times he slapped it down, and the black-brown body still heaved and juddered in its dying. I hated that sound, that wet slap of flesh onto rock, that frantic flapping of a body shocked and hurt out of its medium.

I was watching him too closely; my line snagged far out among the rocks, my silver bait hooked in rock or seaweed. I tugged; the gut stretched with me, stuck again. I called to him, and he took the rod, jerked it this way and that, but nothing gave.

"I'll wade out after it, see if I can free it that way."

I held the rod; he guided himself out with the line; his waders came right up as far as his hips; soon the base of his jacket was tipping the water, a low wave reached over the rim of his waders and he jerked backwards; "It's too deep for the waders", he called back, "I can't reach it."

He came ashore and took off his jacket; then he took the waders off, his socks, and then his trousers. He was wearing white woollen shorts underneath the trousers; he took that off, too, never glancing in my direction; I stood, dumbfounded. He tucked his shirt up inside its top buttons, exposing his body from his shoulderblades to his toes. He took hold of the line again and followed it out into the sea.

He stood at the edge of the world, Father, naked, and I choked into silence, watching his white body move out into the ocean, feeling the action of his fingers on the line, the sun setting away to our right, the sea gentle about us. I remember the marks of the elastic tips of his underpants about his waist, a white softening of the flesh there; I remember the way the bones of his lower spine showed through the flesh, how the buttocks were beginning to wrinkle, the white valleys of his lower back, the blue and purple veins of his thighs. He moved in the water, cautious of his foothold.

By the time he got to the rocks where the hook was caught the water was up to his chest, the shirt at his back was trailing. I could see the jerk of the line as it came free. He gave a cry of satisfaction, held the bait high over his head, like a trophy, and waved to me. Then he turned to come in.

"I've a fish! I've a fish!" I shouted, pretending to grip hard on the rod, bending backwards with the strain of it. The line was taut between us, my naked father coming up from the ocean. He came ashore, and again I was stunned as he rose towards me out of the water. The strength of his chest, coloured red and blue and purple, the navel almost disappearing in the hang of his stomach, the dark, surprising hair of his crotch, the soft, small lie of his penis, the shrivelled purse of his testicles.

"Landed," he said, "thanks be to God…"

There was no word of complaint, no reproach.

"Thanks," I said, stammering at him, "you're great."

He was shivering. It was growing dark. He hopped about on the shore to dry off, to warm up. I noticed the laughter of the gulls, the sharp, sudden cry of a curlew, the distant barking of a dog. The sun dropped suddenly off the shelf at the far edge of the horizon and the sea stilled under a rare calm. We stood between day and night, my naked father watching far out to sea, watching somewhere very far beyond me. There was a sudden splash and a sea-trout soared in an arc into the air and dropped again. The man sighed and turned back towards the world.

MATTHEW

MY ABIDING MEMORY OF THAT TIME IS OF WEATHER. MORNING after morning I struggled with the bike, against winds and rains; I was wrapped up in all sorts of wind cheaters but by the time I reached Saint Joseph's I was exhausted, and runnels of rain were falling from me. I was often late, too, and scolded and had to spend the first half-hour steaming by the schoolroom fire.

Brother Heaney came into class one day, said the prayers very slowly, pausing a long while in silence before blessing himself. We stood, still as stones, afraid to upset the silence he had created about us. Then he asked us to step out of our desks and kneel down on the floor because he wanted our full and total attention. We knelt, clumsily, there was a clattering against desks, books tumbled, there was a lot of shuffling and glancing about. Brother Heaney stood and waited, hands joined over the soutane, deep blue eyes watching us.

"Join your hands, boys, in prayer; learn once again of the perfidy, the treachery of our foe! Just a few mornings ago, my dear boys, England added another crime to her already overlong list of crimes against our poor country. They have made martyrs of our 1916 heroes; they have done to death the lord mayor of Cork; now they have murdered a child, a boy scarcely older than yourselves. And of what was this young boy guilty that he had to be murdered by these cowards? he was guilty, boys, as I am guilty, as you are guilty, of a longing to free his country from centuries of tyranny, to drive the invader out of his land. No more than that, boys, no more than that.

"There was an ambush, above in Dublin; a group of Volunteers, of whom this boy was one, attacked a lorry supplying bread to the enemy. An English soldier died in the course of his duty, boys, in the course of what was for him merely his duty. Our young boy, Kevin his name was, Kevin Barry, was found with a revolver in his hands, and he was arrested. Two and two in Ireland come to four. But when the English do the sum what do they get? Five. That's what they get. They accused the boy of murdering the British soldier. They took him to prison and beat him brutally in his cell and brought him before their own, ill-conceived and sinful court and condemned him to death. Without proof! Or proper trial! And is this to be a soldier's death? No, no, boys! They hanged him, they hanged him on the gallows, he was murdered by the common hangman in the name of English justice!"

My knees hurt against the wooden floor; I looked up to see Brother Heaney; he had his handkerchief to his nose and he blew into it, quickly, then wiped the gathering tears away. Behind him was the blackboard on its easel, the grey ghosts of knowledge hovering; behind that, on the wall over the fire-place, a picture of Jesus Christ, the Crucified. Brother Heaney put his handkerchief up the sleeve of his soutane and began again. I dropped my head.

"The hangman's rope was dropped round this young man's neck, the noose perfect, tested, tried, the slip-knot professionally done. He held his head high, this young son of Ireland, and he looked his Maker in the eye. They tortured our Saviour, our Christ, and they tortured Kevin Barry. Little more than a child, the people pleading for his life. But the invaders demanded blood, a sacrifice, and his blood shall be upon them, boys, and upon all their works."

Brother Heaney's voice had risen until he was close to

shouting. Now we were all watching him, there was fire in my soul at his words, rage against the intruders, a willingness to spend my life, too, in the great struggle for freedom.

"Kneel erect now boys, kneel erect. We will pray together to the great Master; we will pray that Kevin Barry's sacrifice shall not go in vain, that his name and honour will be remembered wherever walks a true Irish son, we will pray that the blood spilled from Kevin Barry's body may flow in a river of pleading before the great Lord who gave His own blood for all of us on Calvary. In the name of the Father, and of the Son, and of the Holy Ghost ..."

I thought of Kevin Barry as I cycled home, battling the wind, tears of frustration and effort mingling with the rain. I climbed down from the bike and began to push it along beside me. I imagined myself, like Barry, stepping out on the boards of the gallows, hands tied behind my back, crowds below me, gazing up, murmuring with sympathy and admiration as I took my place on the floor of the world – the pride, the self-consciousness, the absolute certainty of my definition. And then the fear, the view of the rope, the noose, the sense of it harsh against my neck, touching the Adam's apple, pressing against the back of my head ...

I thought, too, of Terence Mac Swiney, of my betrayal. And I thought of Stephen Connors, his sacrifice, his smile, his pride. Must it always be like this? The scapegoat, the sacrifice, the breaking of bodies so that others may live more safely? No change brought about unless blood is spilt? And then – a thought struck me. I laughed out loud into the wind and gathering darkness. Perhaps I could arrange a blood-sacrifice of my own to force a change for the better in my situation ... Ahead of me the great slope downwards of Drisheen Hill. My decision taken I mounted again, not allowing myself any further space for thought, and I set off as quickly as the wind would let me.

The bike gathered momentum as I raced down the hill. To my left was the ditch with furze bushes everywhere. To my right a deep drain, overgrown with grass and brambles, and beyond the drain another ditch running along someone's humpy acres. I decided on the drain, as offering a greater possibility of damage to the bike and a lesser degree of possibility of major injury to myself. I screamed a long, high scream as I turned the bike towards the drain.

At the last moment I lost my nerve and tried to bring the bike to a stop. I jammed on both front and rear brakes. But I was going too fast. The bike skidded along the road, turned to the side and slewed sickeningly against the verge, flinging me off against the ditch where I tumbled into the drain below. Then there was silence. Only wind and the sound of rain. And the ticking of the front wheel still spinning slowly.

There was a sharp pain in my right shoulder. I could feel the dampness of the drain begin to seep into me where I lay; there were stinging pains and dull sores beginning to push themselves into my consciousness from several parts of my body. I was still some two miles from home. With great difficulty I extracted myself from the bike, the brambles, the water. My bag had burst open and there were books and copies afloat on the green mess of the drain. My feet were deep in mud as I tried to gather things up; the pain in my shoulder was intense. I threw everything down, clambered onto the road and began to walk, a wounded hero, homewards.

Eventually I was hauling myself among the few houses of Drumdouglas. It was cheering to see lamplight through the windows, to get the wonderful aroma of cooking bacon, and mutton, to see grey ghosts rise above the chimneys and be whisked away into the air. Then I was out past McGlynn's pub and the darkness was complete again. I sat down on the low ditch by Harte's meadows and thought I'd like to take root there, so little will had I left to do the last mile. To take root like a lopped branch, be passive before the elements, have wooden thoughts, ideas like knots in timber, no more questions, no blood-sacrifices! Only when I heard a rustling sound among the trees near Harte's big front gates, a sound I interpreted as that of a cloven-hoofed monster out of Hell, watching me, did I scare myself enough to up and on again.

I got home. I stood before the door a while, wiping my hands on my sodden coat, wiping my face as clean as I could of tears and blood and slime, waiting to put a face on myself before my father. I opened the door. Thomas laughed out loud when he saw me; Delia, fussing at the table with plates and things, stared stupidly; Father was sitting at the fire, working on the wicker weaving of a creel; he looked up, spat into the fire, and went back to his work; but I detected the small light of a grin somewhere behind his face, and I knew I would be safe. Mother, her hands rubbing water from the sink into her old apron, came fussing and clucking towards me. I was safe, home, in my own place, the great scent of boxty bread sweeping me up in its fat arms.

My small blood sacrifice worked! My shoulder was sprained and I developed a severe cold that kept me at home for days. Father took out the cart and brought home my bike; the front wheel was buckled, the chain snapped, even the crossbar had been bent. Several spokes had come out from the back wheel and were bent and twisted every which way. Under Mother's quiet persistence, he admitted that it may be too much to have to cycle over and back in Winter the long distance to Saint Joseph's. He sat himself down by the fire to brood. History's hero lay in bed in the lower room.

DAVID

I FIND IT DIFFICULT TO IMAGINE THEIR LOVE-MAKING; MY OWN entrance into the dream, my stirring in what black mud of absence, my springing to attention in anticipation of the climax. The big, front bedroom, crowded with wardrobe, dressing-table, the great bed. The window with its bay-seat, large panes, sashes, window-cords, the heavy curtains.

The big Pye Radio must have been loud with the War, those terrible events, gigantic slaughtering that went on daily somewhere across the seas, but whose echoes reached even to the remote west of Ireland. The sky was thick with it. Blood making the earth slippery, acres and acres of earth, in France, in Germany, In Turkey, in Russia, in North Africa, in England ... drenching the ground the way a thunderstorm drenches the clay of our garden. Drenching souls. Their hopes for the fruition of goodness.

I can imagine his gentleness, his concern that she, too, participate in the pleasure of the act of love. But I see only a darkened room, the curtains that reach down to the floor drawn tight, the looming furniture, sheets and blankets and eiderdown and already a sense of guilt, she keeping herself distant from him, he too barely making something of the moment. Outside, the dullness of an afternoon on a landscape that slopes away from their upstairs window, over a stone wall, over humpy, barren soil splotched with heathers, across thin meadows raw with rushes, all greens and browns, dampness and infertility, down to the muddy foreshore.

Perhaps those of us conceived and born during the great

hatreds of that War have hoped that we carry within us a
greater longing for love and peace than mankind knew
before? Perhaps somewhere in us is the awareness that we
have learned so much of war we cannot let it ever happen
again? On the strand of a surging ocean of blood I came to
life – out of the groins and risen penis of this strange being
stretched in his agony before me, out of the dark depths
that were the womb of my mother – and I came ashore,
blood-covered, to search for my own space and location,
my mouth filled with blood, my eyes stopped by blood,
love in my heart, a panting after peace in my soul.

He has been moving
on the widening circumference
of a circle of his own making;

eye bright, back straight, and head erect;
his shirt-sleeves folded, sweat on his flesh,
intoxicating clover-pollen, daisy-dust,

rising to him, and the high grass –
in breathless ballet – falling at his feet;
he has achieved a rhythm

that takes him from us for a while,
his soul a hub of quietness,
his body melting into the almost perfect

elliptical orbiting of the world;
soon he will flop down tiredly amongst us,
his thoughts, as after sex, moving

on the heroes of myth and literature
while the grass at the centre of his circle
has begun, imperceptibly, to green.

MATTHEW

AFTER THE CHRISTMAS BREAK THE NEW YEAR DAWNED WITH A
million question marks across its face. Father took out the
horse and trap and brought me to St Joseph's. The first
question was being answered. Manus came, too, that first
day, for the easy ride into school. His eyes were wide
open, wondering at my suitcase with its old belt keeping it
tight, my clean, new clothes, perhaps, too, the smugness
that must have been written all over my face.

We set off after breakfast, Father sitting up on the trap,
holding the reins, calling out:

"Yup there, yup! yup there, yup! yup there, yup!"

It was a song in the dimness of that winter morning,
like the clanging rhythm of the Drumdouglas-Cloyne train
that went puffing down the line past us, faces peering out,
carriages swaying gently, steam coughing into the air above
the engine:

"Yup there, yup! yup there, yup! yup there, yup!"

Manus and I sat on cushions, jolted, hopping about in
our laughter, though I made every effort to keep my new
clothes clean. Occasionally we'd get off and run alongside
to warm up again as the mare trotted. Slow dawning, mist
chilling us, frost clinging to the fields. Drumdouglas village
drowsed on, turfsmoke hanging above the chimneys like
grey twine tying the houses to Heaven. No sign for many a
day of the English murderers though we had our list
pinned up inside the door at home: how many in the
house, sex, age, occupation – just in case of a sudden,

military inspection. At times Father disappeared for days, the gun disappearing with him. And we did not ask questions.

"Yup there, yup! yup there, yup! yup there, yup!"

I was given a small room in St Joseph's and treated with respect by the other boys. I was now a guest of the Christian Brothers, my education in their hands, my future promised to them in return. I got home for holidays, of course, and the prayers and devotions I had to say were, for the time being, undemanding. Quickly, however, among the gentle fervour of those men, my purpose hardened, my sense of the great service they performed quickening my resolve, urging me on, like the train on its track, like the old mare responding to the voice:

"Yup there, yup! yup there, yup! yup there, yup!"

At the end of that first year in St Joseph's all talk was of the truce; it seemed, after so many centuries, that England was going to allow us space in which we could be free. The Summer was a wonderful one; there was sunshine almost every day; our hearts were full of pride for the way we had taken part in the war for independence. Father stalked his fields with new purpose. Manus Cafferky and I went fishing together and the tiny fish we caught were richer than ever before because they were our fish, truly ours. We spent a day at Cafferky's, helping to get the hay in, Thomas, Delia and I, with my father and Manus, even Mr Cafferky came out into the meadows and hobbled about on his crutches, giving orders, enjoying himself hugely.

Meanwhile, they were talking in London. Those whom we had revered as heroes were now full of words and arguments, news filtering through to us in Drumdouglas, slowly. The Brothers spoke a lot among themselves, they seemed as uncertain about things as we were. It was a year of silence; we heard of treaties with the English, of oaths of allegiance to the Crown, and the Brothers grew irritable; we heard of splits, of Collins talking to the enemy, of de Valera sitting somewhere at home, plotting ... and the Brothers got heated during mealtimes, and someone mentioned the awful words *Civil War* and those who had fought and won now seemed to be lining up on one side of a wall, and those who had fought and won, too, were lining up on the other side of the wall. And at home, during the holidays, I heard some of the men talking again of their guns, and I knew the blood lust was rising from the earth all over again.

Manus Cafferky and I were in the same class in St Joseph's, though he still cycled to and fro every day while I stayed warm and snug in the Brothers' house. I spent several evenings in the Cafferky house during the Easter holidays, trying to work out a Latin text with Manus. We were on some piece of manoeuvring by Julius Caesar, some slaughtering of the Germans, or quelling of barbarians outlined with mathematical precision. Mr Cafferky was sitting on his stool, smoking, watching us, an indulgent smile on his face.

For some reason I stopped and looked up at Mr Cafferky; it seemed like quite a natural comment for me to make at the time, and I said:

"Mr Cafferky, my father has taken out his gun again, as if all we did and suffered had not happened."

The smile left his face with awful suddenness. He took the pipe out of his mouth and sat up, sharply, on his stool. He was going to say something, then changed his mind and began scraping at the bowl of his pipe, hiding his face from me. I could see the rough bandages still around his leg, the crutch leaning against the wall by the fireplace. Manus was looking at me. I shrugged my shoulders and got back to the destruction of the Germans. We did a chapter or two of the book and then, without warning, Mr

Cafferky flung his pipe against the wall where it smashed into pieces. I looked at him; he was trembling, his hands bunched in great fists and he had gone pale as milk. He turned towards me; and then he said, with a slowness and quietness not to be argued with:

"Matthew Blake," he said, "you must leave this house now and you must not come back here again. Do you hear me? You are not welcome in this house. Go now, go!"

I was overwhelmed. I looked over at Manus. He shook his head ever so slightly and turned away from me. It was not the time for questions. I gathered up the books that belonged to me and I left the Cafferky house, walking down the lane towards the main road the way a ghost must drift hopelessly through the world he has left and can neither leave nor re-enter.

My father said:

"Matt, you know what's going on in Dublin and London? Collins has been talking to the English and selling away what we fought for over so many years. They have this treaty drawn up, imagine that! with the enemy, and instead of holding on to the freedom we have won, they are selling it away and swearing to take an oath of allegiance to that same crown. De Valera has abandoned them to their pigsty; they are grunting and rooting about in their own mess but de Valera, Liam Lynch and many more true men have not agreed to parcel out our country and live in the same sty as the English. There are those who follow Collins, who believe the English will think that the freedom we have won is only a first step and that we can beg for more freedom later on. That's what it means, Matt, they will ask the English to give us, please, another inch! And Donal Cafferky, in spite of that leg that they gave him as a gift, is willing to lie down before them and lick their boots! Not us, Matt, not us! We will fight for the Republic we have fought for over all the years. There is a war coming, Matt, a war between Irishman and Irishman, and England knows it, and England wants it, and when it happens the English will saunter back in to our country, and they will be laughing and they will make slaves of us all once again. But not without a fight, Matt, not without a fight! Not with de Valera there to lead us!"

From then on, Manus Cafferky and I sat one at the North pole and one at the South pole in the class. Soon we were not even looking at one another. Sometime in April the Republicans took over the Four Courts in Dublin; the Brothers shook their heads, they were worried. Then, around the beginning of the Summer holidays, the Provisional Government troops stormed the Four Courts and the Civil War had begun, for sure. That was the Summer when my father was away from home most of the time, when the Staters came down on us from Dublin, the Irregulars fighting a hopeless battle. Once more the flying columns, father among them, lived on and off in the mountains, mined bridges and set ambushes, like children fighting adults for possession of their tiny fields.

Mid-morning, one of those September days, the classroom door sprang open; Brother Hughes was teaching us mathematics at the time; I remember a jumble of calculations on the blackboard, their irrelevance to the broken figure that appeared at the door behind the superior, Brother Hines. He was a small man, dressed in a dark trench coat, a hat pulled down over his forehead, darkening his face. He was stooped and furtive looking. Brother Hines addressed Brother Hughes, but the speech was meant for us all.

"Brother," he said, "please forgive the intrusion. But it is a matter of some importance. This gentleman is one of the Irregulars, fighting for the restoration of the Republic. He has been involved in some sort of business out at

Knockreidy Cross where several of his companions have
been taken. The army of the Provisional Government is in
pursuit. He has asked us to shelter him for some few days.
It will be an act of mercy, Brother, to do so, I am sure you
will agree, and it will be an act of kindness and concern
for a fellow Irish patriot that we should do everything in
our power to protect one of our own. Therefore," and he
turned very deliberately towards us, "I am expecting every
boy in this room, no matter what his personal convictions
may be, to respect the freedom of an Irishman to seek
sanctuary amongst the Christian Brothers. I shall demand
nothing more from you, boys, than your silence, should
you be questioned about this incident. But your silence I
shall demand, indeed, boys, I shall command your total
and complete silence on this event until this terrible war
shall have come to an end."

Brother Hines was a big man, muscular, middle-aged
and stern; there was nobody who would go against him
when he made a statement like that. The man in the trench
coat stood behind him, shaking a little; he was wet
through, as if he had been out in a heavy shower though
the day was crisp and still and dry. Just then we heard the
sound of lorries on the gravel drive outside the school;
Brother Hines began to usher the Irregular through a door
that looked like a small cupboard door at the top, left-hand
corner of the classroom; there was a storeroom behind the
door, used to keep classroom materials. Then he lifted the
blackboard over in front of the door and motioned to
Brother Hughes to work at it. Brother Hines left our room.

We buried our heads in our books. Outside we could
hear boots on the stone floors of the corridors, on the
wooden floors of the classrooms, voices loud in
questioning and command. Brother Hughes tried to follow
a line of discourse concerning the marks on the
blackboard. Fugitive little-animal tracks across a waste-

land. I glanced back to where Manus was sitting; for a
moment I caught his eye. He looked away quickly. The
door sprang open and two Staters came in, dressed in the
uniform of the provisional army.

They looked about the room. One of them asked
Brother Hughes if any outside person had been in the
classroom. Brother Hughes answered with indignation:

"How dare you! How dare you, young man, burst into a
room where young boys are studying for their exams, as if
you owned the school, as if you had never attended a
school yourself, as if you had never learned the good
manners and customary graces that all these young boys
know instinctively. How dare you, sir, how dare you!"

The Stater was taken aback. He half saluted, and took
hesitant steps away from the Brother. The other Stater had
moved down along the class; he held a rifle in both hands,
its barrel pointed at an angle towards the ceiling. He was
watching us, his eyes moving rapidly, a small smile playing
about his lips. Oh yes, this was a cute one, sharp,
dangerous. I met his eyes for just a moment, but I noticed
that Manus kept his head very low and for a moment the
Stater paused beside his desk. He poked him ever so
gently with the butt of his gun and Manus looked up with
a guilty start.

"Well?" the Stater asked him, quietly, "don't be afraid,
young man, what do you know that would interest us?"

Manus gulped and looked around awkwardly from boy
to boy; he did not look in my direction. For a moment I
felt certain he was going to inform and my whole soul
screamed for the hidden Irregular, and for Manus, too. I
spoke out, loudly and firmly.

"There was someone came running through the yard at
breaktime this morning, I saw him, a man in a coat, I didn't
know who he was, he went through the yard, out through
the farm buildings, over the fence on the other side. I think

he was heading for the mountains. There's a shed out there on Bunnageera and I got the idea he was going up there."

Brother Hughes backed me up.

"Matt!" he shouted at me. "How often have I told you not to speak until you're asked! Stand out there by the wall at once. We'll deal with you when these men apologise for this unwarranted intrusion and take their leave of us."

The Stater grinned; he winked at me, nodded and said, "Thanks, young fella, you're a true Irishman."

Then they left the classroom, closing the door violently after them. We heard voices shouting in the corridor; there was a great deal of running, of doors banging; then we heard the sound of engines starting up and of vehicles moving off over the gravel. Silence returned slowly. Nobody stirred. At last Brother Hughes began to giggle, quietly.

"Nice one, Matt," he said, "nice one."

I was proud of myself at that moment. I looked over at Manus, I could see that he was livid, trembling with anger, gripping the sides of his desk with violence.

The fight between us was inevitable after that. I stood in the yard at lunchtime that day, and Manus, with some of his friends, stood at the other end. I watched across the yard at that broad back and I knew the wall between us would have to be cracked. He turned suddenly, as if he had sensed my eyes on him. Several boys were playing with a ball around the yard; there was the usual screeching and bantering all around us. Manus finished eating his lunch; he wiped his mouth and spoke quietly with his friends. I moved from my place and Manus moved towards me, his friends following. There was an immediate silence around the yard.

"I was trying to give you a way out, Manus," I called to him.

"Since when did I need your help?" he answered.

I flung it at him. "When your father was besieged up in your house by the Tans, that's when!"

He flinched from that. But he shouted: "And who killed Michael Collins then?"

I laughed. "How do I know who killed Michael Collins? I certainly didn't."

"No, but de Valera and your bloody Republican Irregulars did."

"And who took prisoners out to blow them up with bombs?"

"Nobody did that. They planted the bombs; they couldn't defuse them. They were too stupid."

"All this is getting us nowhere. We were on the same side, once."

"We were; it's you who have split away, gone against any chance we ever had of peace."

"What good is peace when you have to lick the arse of the enemy to keep that peace?"

We had come very close now, almost face to face, squaring up to one another, willing on the fight, hoping for it. He pushed me quickly in the chest and I took a step backwards. I pushed him, then, and he drew back his fist and struck at me. I bent away from the blow and he stumbled against me. I grappled him and flung him to the ground behind me as he stumbled. First blood to me!

Such fights are never what they appear to be in films, in comics, on TV. There are none of the prancings and squarings, no neat upper-cuts, jabs, foot-magic, of boxing; these are crude, grabbing, reaching, swinging affairs, based on rough strength, fear, and luck. We wrestled awkwardly, falling, tearing ourselves and our clothes against the rough earth of the yard, soiling hands and faces, shirts and trousers with clay and blood; oh yes, there is always blood, nose-bleeds, knuckles cut, sometimes a lucky blow will strike beneath the eye, open a cut. Blood-sacrifice again!

We crossed the yard, hurt, unhappy, our hands flailing, even our feet, our boots, striking out whenever possible. He fell over and I fell on top of him and we wrestled and scuffled on the ground. Then I was up again and aimed a kick at his ribs when he was struggling to get up; I caught him on the arm instead and he roared with the pain of it. He rushed into me, his head lowered, charging me the way a goat will charge, and he took my breath away, catching me in the midriff. I held onto him and pushed and heaved against him until he was up against the wall of a shed. His head was still against my stomach and I held him that way, bringing up my knee into his face. He jerked upwards and I slammed him back against the wall. Suddenly I was grabbed powerfully from behind and pulled away. It was Brother Hines. He caught me by the collar of my shirt; then he caught Manus and pulled and dragged us by the sheer force of his big manhood, into the hallway of the school.

We stood, one on either side of him, bleeding, filthy, sweating, panting. I felt right was mine; that Brother Hines would be on my side; I tried to hold my head up proudly. But I found it hard to get my breath, I needed to wipe my face clean of its blood and sweat and mucous.

"St Joseph's is not the place for such brawls!" Brother Hines roared at us. I looked up at him, surprised. "We are living through terrible times, terrible, wicked times. I do not know, and I do not care, what side of this awful division either of you is on. What I care about is this! that there shall be no working out of your antagonisms in this school. That is for outside school. Am I understood?" He screamed the last words at us both and we instantly answered, "Yes, Brother."

Without another word he took out a cane he kept inside his black soutane. He turned first to Manus.

"Manus Cafferky," he announced, "I am punishing you for fighting in this school. Fighting is not allowed and any boy caught fighting is to be punished. Is that clear?"

"Yes, Brother."

Brother Hines administered six strokes of the cane on each of Manus's palms. Manus winced from the blows, his whole body imploding with the shock and pain, his face screwed up in agony. Tears came quickly to his eyes and rolled down his face, but he did not shout, or cry out. I winced with him, and I cringed before my own impending suffering.

"You, Matthew Blake," said Brother Hines, turning towards me. "I am punishing you for fighting in the school. Fighting in the school is not allowed. Is that clear?"

I, too, received six strokes on each palm. I bent and withdrew from the blows as well as I could, but my flesh was quivering. I counted, oh so awfully slowly, four, right hand, four, left hand, five, right hand … and at last it was over. I put my hands in under each armpit, pressing them hard against the warmth of my body, trying to squeeze the pain out of them. But Brother Hines was not finished yet.

"Matthew Blake," he began again. "I am punishing you the more because I expect more from you. You are a privileged student in our school, being cared for and educated by the Brothers. In response more must be asked of you. Do I make myself understood?"

"Yes, Brother." I quailed. I held out my right hand.

Brother Hines administered three more swipes of the cane on each hand. When it was over I fell back against the wall, slid down and ended sitting on the floor. Manus stood on the other side of the hallway, his hands clenched tightly against his belly. Brother Hines strode quickly down the hallway, out the door and back into the yard. I have a very strong recollection of the red and green glass in the panels around the side of that great front door. How the sun shone gently through them. How the world outside must be lovely and at peace. Manus moved slowly towards the door and went out. I remember thinking that nothing had been achieved, wondering how I could ever get up from the floor, if my hands would ever be able to feel the tufts that grow on the tips of rushes, able to play handball again, to shake hands with friends ... And then I cried, loudly and unashamedly, sitting on the stone floor of the hallway of the Christian Brothers' school, morning and evening, another day.

DAVID

I REACHED FORWARD AND HELD HIS HAND; IT LAY, ALMOST perfectly still, on the eiderdown, the pyjama sleeve high on the wrist, the watch ticking away his last hours. I laid my hand over his. There was no reaction; he had moved away into that morass of living, soft and dark and treacherous, between life and death. He was in that space, that time, from which he cannot call back to the world of the living. I wonder if he can yet call forward into the land of the dead? My hand softly on his, like a whisper, a memory, a dream.

That night in Summer. Not quite dark outside. There was a gentle breeze moving in the grove of pine trees. Like ghosts, distraught, sighing. I had the curtains half closed but the bedroom was dark. I had said my night prayers and was trying to get to sleep, imagining all sorts of exciting things to keep my mind off fright and fiends. When I heard the fluttering at the window it was as if a whole balloon of repressed fears had burst inside me and I screamed and screamed.

I heard his footsteps come quickly up the stairs; when he came into the room he brought light with him; I was sitting up petrified, my hand pointing towards the window. He drew back the curtains.

There was a moth, large and grey and downy, worrying itself against the pane. Father smiled, stood back and let me see. I was ashamed. The fluttering of grey-white wings with a tiny pattern of spots, made a noise, as of finger-tapping, against the glass. The head was large, furred with white down, there were long, black feelers frantic in its fright.

Father lowered the top half of the window; he made a saucer of his hands – I remember how they looked, shapely, well-cut fingernails, but strong and brown and touched with dark hairs – and laid it over the creature. He closed his hands about it, making a ball and it became the heart; he held it close to me and I could hear the dreadful panic it must have known in that confined space; I knew, too, how caring a place it was, how safe from predators, how it could rest quietly in that surety. He held his hand close to my ear for a while, that pulsing place, heart-cavern; then he stretched his hands out the window and released the moth; it flew away into darkness, like a word quickly uttered and remembered, a quick sense of whiteness in a black world.

As yet we had not spoken.

"Now," he said, "go to sleep, and think of the moth and how happy it must be to be free again, flying about under the stars."

He was settling me down, tucking sheets and blankets about me; then he laid his right hand gently on my forehead – just that, just once, just for a moment. I must have been asleep before he closed the curtains, and left the room.

Now I trace patterns of veins on a hand gnarled as the trunk of an old ash. There are brown flecks, rust-coloured coins, like old halfpennies he has collected over the years, for the ferryman. And there is no answering warmth from them, no comfort to be found in their touch, now, at last, when I seek it again, and offer it. Where do I turn to, now, where do I go from here?

MATTHEW

TOWARDS THE END OF JANUARY, FATHER, PAT MCKEOWN AND
Jimmy Turley went out to the curve where the railway line
sloped round the valley. On its right, as it headed south,
the wet fields of the valley, on its left a drumlin covered
with scutch grass and ragged shrubs. The train was
bringing troops from the city south. I was lookout. We had
crowbars. A sledgehammer.

As I crouched on the top of the drumlin, my eyes taking
in the main road and the outer reaches of Drumdouglas, I
knew I had been in a similar position before. Gone now
was the excitement, the tingle; all that remained was a
determination, body and mind alert with anger, a sense of
martyrdom, too, because we were beginning to feel we
were mining an abandoned shaft.

The men worked steadily. They lifted a long stretch of
track, shifting it bodily to one side, slightly, so that it would
not be visible from a distance. The tink and clunk of
hammers filled the valley, the sounds of straining crowbars,
the iron resisting, then yielding with a groan. Father
insisted on staying to watch the result of their labours.
McKeown and Turley vanished, back into the village. I was
for going, too, but Father wanted to witness the unfolding
of events. Of course I stayed with him. I had to.

We waited at least an hour. Trains, during that awful
war, did not run to schedules. Too many bridges had been
bombed. Too many ambushes laid. It was freezing, there in
the low scrub; a wind came round the valley from the heart

of winter, its load was ice and snow. I had to rise to shake and jump some warmth back into me. That day did Father no good. He lay, dismissing any suggestion of cold, waiting.

The train, when it came, surprised us, appearing out of trees at the far end of the valley, smoke from its funnel merging with the dark, low clouds. We saw it before we heard its rough coughing. It emerged, a ghost, to haunt us. When I heard it, the clatter of its engine made it mortal again, the slight angle as it lay into the curve made it vulnerable. It hauled three, closed, wagons, we knew they were filled with Staters, possibly with machineguns, definitely with menace.

It approached the broken line with unforgivable slowness. For a while I was convinced someone had noticed the damage though there was no face visible anywhere, from the engine or the wagons. And then it hit. There was a harsh, grinding, iron scream, a long-drawn-out metal cry of woe, as engine and wagons slewed sickeningly along the sleepers and the stones, tearing everything as they went, coming to a halt at a tilt to the line. To our disappointment neither engine nor wagon toppled over. But we had stopped the train. It would take time and suffering to get it back in action. I shouted at Father and I began to run.

He did not move. I came back, urging him. He was trying to rise. I could see he was too stiff to get up. Men had leaped down from the engine of the train; I could see their figures fussing about down in the valley. I could hear the bolts and racket from the wagons as soldiers began to emerge. Father was so stiff with cold I had to lift him bodily to his feet. We turned to get down the hill. He stumbled and fell; I could not hold him up. I heard voices shouting from the valley. I hauled him up again. Leaning on me, dragging himself, he made it for a few yards. Then he fell again. He refused to get up.

"Run!" he said, "run! I'm too old for this. There's no chance of me making it. Run! I'll be alright."

He was gazing up at me, his face pale as frosted grass, a smile about his lips but not in his eyes. I refused to leave. I bent down to help him. One more try. He yielded to me and I began to heave him up again. He got on his feet and heeled over immediately.

"I'm frozen to the bone, and my left leg is useless with cramps. I can't stir. Run, Matt! Run, now! GO!"

The voices were louder behind us; there was the sound of a rifle shot, clear and sharp through the chilled air. Father sat down heavily on the ground. I was convinced they had killed him.

"Go!" He began to yell at me. "Go! I'm telling you to go, Matt. They mustn't get you. Go! Run!"

I ran, bobbing and weaving, expecting to know the fire of a bullet in my back. I remember thinking how it was said the sound of the shot travelled more slowly than the bullet itself. As you fell you'd hear the shot. But I made it, into a small clump of trees not far from the main road. I turned. The Staters, about ten of them, were on top of the hill, outlined against the grey-white midday sky. They had their guns raised and were coming towards Father. I backed away through the trees, I was crying furiously, blinding myself, angry, in despair.

Father was taken to Tralee barracks where he spent about a week. They took him out once with others and he had to work to defuse a bomb somewhere. But he survived. He was taken to Kilmainham Gaol in Dublin. He survived that, too. He went on hunger strike for a time. He survived. I stayed at home from St Joseph's and tried to keep us all alive. There were reports of executions. And one by one the Republican leaders were destroyed. When Liam Lynch was shot, trying to escape among the scrub and scutch grass of Knockmealdown mountain, it all seemed hopeless. De Valera too, was locked into Kilmainham Gaol. He also survived. That was as close as my father ever came to Eamon de Valera.

DAVID

THE NURSES, ALL STARCH AND BUSY-NESS AND PLAINNESS, USHERED us out; they would be just a few minutes, scarcely longer; they would make him more comfortable now, they would bathe him and change his pyjamas after the long night. I remained, there had been too many silences between us all those years, too many distances. The head nurse shrugged. Then she nodded, smiling at me.

They drew the curtains firmly about the bed, they lifted his unyielding weight and with some difficulty removed his pyjamas. They slipped a rubber sheet under his white, suffering flesh, and ever so gently, with practised skill, they bathed him, sponging him with warm water, dabbing him dry with white, soft towels, touching him deftly, the straggling grey hairs of his armpits, the down-like hairs on his chest, the scarred hollow of his stomach, the still, small stables of his testicles with the tiny protection of pubic hair, the long, arched length of his legs, the white, small, perfect feet.

They turned him on one side and bathed his back, down the great breadth of it, down across the levelled valley of his buttocks, into the delicate hollow of the hocks; they turned him then on his other side, bathing and soothing and drying him. Then they took away the rubber sheet and generously sprinkled his body with a small snowstorm of talc, baby powder, their kind, female hands spreading it under his arms, across his chest, all over.

They whispered to an orderly who covered his chin and cheeks with a white lather, and with a straight razor removed it all again, taking with it the small stubble of beard that had come overnight. He bathed the face with a warm cloth, parting the small folds of flesh about the neck, shaving and cleansing as he could. He nicked the flesh, ever so slightly, once, twice, then again, and tiny stains of blood appeared. These he soothed away.

He helped the nurses lift the body and miraculously they put a perfect sheet under him. They dressed him in fresh pyjamas and drew another perfect sheet over him. Then the blanket, then the thin blue quilt. They made a bright summer's day for him, and one of them, touching his face with the very tips of her fingers, seemed to seek, or offer, blessing. She dabbed some aftershave onto her hand and rubbed it kindly onto his skin. She stood back to gaze at him. He was ready, prepared to meet whatever there was to be met; cleansed from the great wrack of the sea he was ready, lying on the shore, and waiting.

He was, as she could see, a gentleman. His eyes closed, his breathing rough, a little eased now. She was young, the nurse, still hopeful of life. She saw the fine scope of his forehead, the few grey hairs left him, she saw the tiny stars of blood under his chin and suddenly, although she was a nurse and he a patient, she kissed him, touching her moist lips to his forehead, breathing a prayer for him to her own, scarcely known, deity. His eyes, I fancied, flickered. She did not know if he was aware of her, if he had caught a glimpse of her. There was no expression on his face, only the ongoing determination of the will to maintain for a while longer the awful labour of living. I saw tears come to the edge of her eyes. She coughed quietly, glanced at the watch on her uniform – 10.20 – smiled in embarrassment at her companion, and left.

The second nurse, apparently unmoved, opened the

curtains a little and beckoned.

"There we are now," she said to nobody in particular, "he's all cleaned and polished, saucered and blowed, as thcy say, dressed to kill, fit to meet beggarman or king. Powdered and perfumed as well as any new-born babe. Like an infant, new-born, new-born ..." And her clacketing heels could be heard as she left the ward. Oh the world! round and round we go, baby to boy to man, to boy to baby to ...

Before they crowded back around him I reached out my hand to him again, to touch him. And hesitated, remembering the ferry, that day, between Achill and Clare.

The waves between the islands
were dark green walls
rising against us;

I cried aloud with the thrill of it,
the throbbing vessel hoisted high
and held – while we watched a moment

towards our fall, that
lurching helplessness down down down;
his face was bright with merriment, his glasses

wet from sea-spray;
sea-birds, auk and guillemot and shearwater
insolent, in their element, about us;

too soon we had reached harbour, the boat
juddering clouds of silt through the clear water,
dull thud of wooden taffrail against concrete;

I grew nervous then of his big body
stepping out between gunwale and pier,
my small hand stretched up uselessly to help;

shorefall, the pale road upwards,
distances, and waves between the islands
rising again between us.

THREE

MATTHEW

I WAS SIXTEEN. I HAD ONE SUITCASE, THE SAME OLD ONE, TIED round with twine. As the train hammered and smoked its way across the fields, peeking in at the backs of houses, I felt for the first time the strange, mesmeric power of the wheels. I was jolted about a great deal, but I was able to settle into a half-dream state with the motion of the wheels, so that the countryside blurred, the way my father and mother, Thomas and Delia had blurred as I waved to them from the train; they stood in a group, and waved, but my tears took them from me, a small group merging into one another, into one, shimmering mass of family.

Wheels, round and round in the eternal game.

The train drew in to the station in Limerick. Everything seemed confused, carriage doors banging, porters calling, pushing trolleys, people shouting, trains waiting, steam escaping in big hisses as if impatient of delay, anxious, like horses, to be off. I got my directions. The train for Dublin! The name filled me with misgivings and excitement. A city, crowded with people rushing and wheeling and confident! and I, a young man, alone, beginning a life among them.

I remember nothing of the journey through a country growing ever stranger to me. At one stage a gentleman came into the carriage and sat down; there was a smell from him, a perfume, he was dressed in clothes to astonish, yellow waistcoat like a huge daffodil growing from his chest, great silver watch he often drew from his fob, grey hat he left beside him on the seat, how he picked it up and turned it round between his hands; he smiled at me, a big, confident smile. Businessman, rich and successful, certain and hurried. I dozed, trusting to the truth of what I was heading for.

When I arrived in Dublin, at Kingsbridge Station, Brother Hamill was there to meet me. As I passed in a daze through the barrier, I noticed him, and he noticed me. He was dressed, of course, in black, black coat covering black suit, and he wore a black hat. People gave way to him with pleasing deference, and he led me quickly out onto the street, through a reel and ruck of vehicles racing about, carriages and trams and cars, honking, growling, rushing, jostling ...

I saw the great walls of the brewery, there were Churches everywhere, spires rising into the evening sky, flocks of starlings crossing the air above them, heading back out into country to roost. With a pang of loneliness I envied them, longed to turn and go back through the night, back to my own place, where I belonged. But Brother Hamill had my suitcase, he had me firmly by the elbow and was guiding me across a bridge over the Liffey, towards a tram.

We took two trams to get to our destination. People jumped on and off, changing places, shuffling, standing looking into themselves. I sat in silence, and Brother Hamill made only a few comments. The noise of the tram was wonderful, bells tinkling, sparks leaping on the wires overhead, lights coming on as we crossed a bridge. Brother

Hamill caught my shoulder and pointed up the street as we crossed; there was a monument reaching higher than any spire I had seen, tall in authority and strength.

"Nelson's Column!" Brother Hamill announced with a smile. "The centre of Dublin, but not its heart, no, no, not its heart!"

We took another tram out along the seafront and then walked for perhaps half an hour along a road that could have been countryside except for the street-lamps, the pavement, and a few houses back from the road. Then we turned off that road and there we were, Brother Hamill fumbling with the keys of a great door in the face of a very large building, black and louring over me in the darkness. Baldoyle. My first step towards a new life. The mouth in the great, black building opened and I was swallowed up.

I woke to the sound of gulls, a sound that broke slowly on my consciousness and brought with it an overwhelming sense of loneliness. The big windows of the dormitory were grey in the early light. There were boys sleeping all around me. I crept across the wooden floor to one of the windows and could just make out the sea about a mile away. In the big garden below the window there were gulls squabbling, there were starlings rushing busily through the dew, and every so often a big gull would fly close to the window, screeching angrily. I felt I was on a ship moving very, very slowly through a vast ocean. I crept back into bed and cried quietly to myself.

The three months I spent in Baldoyle are a blur in my mind. It was not that much different from St Joseph's, the same classes, the same subjects, the same exercises, copybooks, pens, exams looming at the end of term. But now this examination was more than just a test in subjects, passing it meant you were worthy to place yourself in God's presence, failing it suggested your heart was not with God at all. We had to be up very early, wash in cold water at the taps, keep silence, behave like fledgling saints. Feather-soft. Our minds on things aloft. Our hearts fixed on the invisible.

Peter Andrew Woods was almost the same age as me, he was big, with a fine shock of black hair, a turnip-coloured face and a sharp sense of humour. We became friendly. One of the few opportunities we had to chat together was during games when we all had to go out onto the pitch for Gaelic football. Rain, snow, frost, or brilliant sunshine with the ground hard as logs we played, eagerly, shedding our frustrations and silences in the rushes of the game. Peter and I played side by side and after every game we chatted. We talked out our loneliness, our sense of confinement at the edge of the city in a big, grey house on the rim of the world.

One day, as we walked from Baldoyle the five miles or so to Dollymount, along the sea-front where the Irish Sea slopped lazily against the stones, Peter Woods frightened me. We were walking together, having managed to hang around and negotiate our positions as we came out of the house. Peter said he could see right across the fields of Baldoyle as far as the railway line that ran between Dublin and Belfast. At about four o'clock every morning he could hear a goods train move slowly through the night, heading for the far north. Often he got up and watched out the window at the lights moving in the distance. It hurt, he said, in strange places of his body and he cried with the grief of it.

"It's only loneliness, Peter," I told him, "and we're all a bit lonely. It's only normal. It'll pass, it'll pass."

After the walk to Dollymount we got in to swim off the rocks at the end of the wall. The great port opened in front of us; here there were bathing places where the water was deep. We splashed about like rowdy urchins and caused

merriment among the sedate people walking on the wall.
Then I noticed Peter, he had swum out a great distance,
slowly and steadily, as if determined to swim away for
ever. His head looked small and his moving arms were tiny
in the distance. The water was cold at the end of summer
and I feared for him. I got out and towelled myself dry,
standing high on the rocks so I could watch him.

All the boys were back on shore and drying themselves
off before it was clear that Peter had turned and was
heading back. He came towards us very slowly and I
admired the steady power of his strokes. We cheered when
he touched the steps and stood up in the water. He waved
his hand but I could see he was very white. He said
nothing and started to dry himself off at once and get
dressed. I made sure to be with him when we set out to
walk back. We walked more quickly now in the late
afternoon, trying to stay warm after the swim. For a long
time Peter was quiet. Then he gripped me by the arm.

"Did you see?" he asked me.

"What?"

"Did you see me swim?"

"Yes, and I was worried about you."

"Ha! so you did notice. I set out to drown myself, Matt.
It just happened. I love swimming. But I felt lonely and
miserable. Something came over me, I went on swimming,
longing to be so exhausted that I'd be taken by the sea and
drowned. I wanted to die, Matt, I wanted to die."

I was silent before the enormity of it. I wanted to grab
Peter and shake him, I wanted to grab him and hug him
and tell him everything would be all right, just hold on,
Peter, just hold on, but somewhere down inside what I
really wanted to say to him was that he should go home
straight away, to his own place. Perhaps they would take
him back without recrimination. And somewhere within
myself I recognised the same urge, the longing to be taken

from the questionable darkness through which we had chosen to walk.

Then one day the superior, Brother O'Hara, called Peter and me into his office. We stood together before his big table and wondered. He got up and came round the table and sat on the edge of it, one leg on the floor, the other dangling; he watched us for a while and I, in my embarrassment, glanced at Peter and giggled.

"So! You think this is funny, Matthew Blake, do you? you think it's all a joke, being here, do you?"

"No, Brother, no."

"Well, I can assure you both that this life is no joke! you are here to join the Christian Brothers and to devote your lives to the education of the children of this country for the honour and glory of God. That, let me assure you, is no joke! That, my fine young friends, is the commitment of a lifetime's labouring in a hard field."

We got a sharp lecture while we stood there, both of us beginning to feel our legs cave in under the pressure of this harangue, yet glad enough while it all remained on the level of distant generalities. He stopped, went back slowly round the table and sat down. He folded his arms on the desk and looked down at his hands. They were immaculate, the nails delicately cut, the half-moons perfect.

"It has come to my attention, Matthew Blake and Peter Woods, that you seem always to be seeking one another out, to want to be in one another's company. Now, things have been wisely structured in this house so that particular friendships will be avoided. Particular friendships, boys, the cleverest ruse the devil has invented to catch our feet. The dangers of particular friendships are many and they will be all outlined to you when you begin your noviciate in some weeks' time. It is, perhaps, one of the greatest dangers facing a Brother, to seek to be always in the company of another Brother. We are for God, boys, for God, we must maintain ourselves pure as the driven snow and keep ourselves always from any hint of temptation. Do you follow me, boys, do you follow me?"

It began to dawn on me, what he was saying, what he was hinting at. I was angry and began to blurt out my concern for Peter when Peter interrupted me, loudly.

"We are very sorry, Brother, we were not aware we were doing wrong. It's my fault. I've been suffering from loneliness and I kept asking Matt for advice. I promise you, I sincerely promise you, it will not happen again."

The determination and seriousness of this little speech were even more disconcerting than anything the Brother had said. I was still angry, however, and I insisted on letting the Brother know that.

"I find it very hard to believe that you would think that kind of thing about us, Brother. I resent ... "

"Matthew Blake! You are not here to resent anything. You are not here to make your feelings known. You are here to become a Brother, a privilege granted to very few. Your lack of humility, your failure to accept correction, constitute a black mark against you. Serve God, Matthew, not your pride! Go now, and may the Lord forgive you your sins!"

As we walked down the corridor towards the study Peter smiled at me and winked, but his face was white and drawn and I knew there was more to it than anything he had said in the Brother's office.

That night Peter Andrew Woods disappeared from the house in Baldoyle. His bed had been slept in but he did not appear at Mass, nor at breakfast, nor at any of the classes during the day. We were not supposed to speak of such things but Peter was the subject of whispered speculations during the day. I heard later that he had taken the boat to Holyhead. He was in Liverpool, he had a job, he was sorry but he couldn't face home after his betrayal ... the disgrace, to himself and his family ... putting his hand to the plough and turning back ...

Brother O'Hara told me these details several days after Peter's disappearance. He quizzed me again and I told him about Peter's suffering, how he had heard the trains ... his swim. Brother O'Hara spoke kindly to me then and talked of my impending grades exam and how he hoped I would soon be heading for the noviciate.

But something had cracked inside of me. What I longed for now was the end of all this study, an end to the unreal world of Baldoyle. I wanted to get away from that place into the actual world of the noviciate where I could put my head down and devote myself with a whole heart and mind to the life of service and dedication that I had chosen. The cries of the gulls continued around the house and they reminded me of Peter. I was restless. The wheel was moving round.

The wheel. And soon it was November. Rains coming across in swathes. All the lights on in the chapel in the early afternoon. Marino. They dressed me in a habit that had belonged to a Brother a good deal bigger than me. The hem came to the ground, made a sweet, brushing sound on the floors of the long corridors of St Mary's. The sleeves reached out over my wrists. I had arrived, commended for my application and seriousness. About my father's business.

The long retreat was a dark, fragrant wood and we mooched about, words like owl-calls, reading the lives of the saints, great, impossible ghosts that had trodden this hard path before us, leaving markers, signposts, headlines too difficult for us to copy, leaving poems we could say by heart but never understand.

Ceremonies beyond ceremonies, someone doing his best on the old, whinging harmonium in the chapel. Eyes down we patrolled the clean corridors, taking in the patterned wooden floors, feeling small and oppressed and ignorant during the silence of mealtimes, the big teapot going round, the monotonous meals of bread and butter and jam, of potatoes and cabbage and bacon.

I sat alone in the chapel one afternoon, crying somewhere far within myself, out of my loneliness. There was no sound. The chapel was small, immaculate, the statues of Joseph and Mary uninspiring. But everywhere the wood was polished to a perfect sheen, the smell of wax lingering on the air. The tiny flame, blood-red, flickered before the altar. Otherwise only the occasional stretching of wood somewhere, the soft distant sigh of stone settling further in the walls, my own breathing loud in my head.

"The end of the Institute is that all its members labour, in the first place for their own perfection; and in the second, for that of their neighbour, by a serious application to the instruction of male children, especially the poor, in the principles of religion and Christian piety."

I tried to force myself inward to find God there. All I could discover was turmoil. Behind me centuries of striving for perfection. Around me walls that had witnessed heroic acts of prayer, devotion and self-immolation. I sighed and sat back on the bench. The sudden creak of timber frightened me. Then I laughed at my own fear and thought of my father, lost too, in a prison cell in this city, alone, yet with others. I knew that de Valera himself was in a cell in the same prison, that there would be the fire of certainty and honour between them, that prisoners whisper through walls that separate them one from another.

I unfolded my arms and sat forward on the bench, careless of any noise I might make, rested my elbows on my knees and buried my face in my hands, closed my eyes and allowed my mind to wander through the fields and hillsides of Drumdouglas, I was a windhover above meadows, hedgerows, woods, I was a fox among undergrowth, around farm-yards, in back lanes, I was a mouse in sheds, haybarns, stables, I was a fly in the rooms of the house, watching Mother knead the dough for apple tarts or mash potatoes for boxty cakes, I could see her lift her head a moment and listen for me, my footstep, my call, or was it for Father she was listening? I opened my eyes and saw the frayed edges of my old soutane, the way its bulk enfolded me, like a shroud, and I cried out loud in that empty place, a long shriek that echoed and re-echoed off wall and roof and floor, startling the saints and angels and God himself with its intensity.

I held on. I survived. And the day came when they gave me a new soutane, fresh and crisp and the correct size, and we were standing together in that same chapel, hearing triumphant music, listening to words of welcome and praise, of heartening and admonishment. And for the first time I heard them announce my new name, Matthew Gonzalez Blake! Brother. I stepped forward and took my place among the others. *Gonzalez!* how could they ... ?

I had some consolation in hearing the names loaded on the shoulders of my companions that day: Celestine, Alban, Otteran, Fidelis, Celsus, Mel, Irenaeus, Maximus, Alphonsus, Munchen ...

Life was hard, very hard, each day a struggle with myself, and with the emptiness I continued to know inside. Whenever it hurt too much I went, alone, into the chapel and remembered my father, and Eamon de Valera, and the prison cells they had to linger in. I was suffering, and so were they. And hadn't Pearse said: *"Bloodshed is a cleansing and sanctifying thing"*, and hadn't we learned that Ireland herself was just like Jesus sacrificed on the Cross? *"Life springs from death, and from the graves of patriotic men and women spring living nations."*

Eamon de Valera, in an issue of "Our Boys" had written of the Brothers:

"You are the children of a noble race and an ancient nation. You will, of yourselves, aspire to be worthy of them, the heirs of love and sacrifice, the issue of generations devoted to the service of Truth and Right, of God and mankind, purified by the sufferings endured and ennobled by the endurance. It is hereditary in you to be true and just and noble – a Kevin Barry or a Terence Mac Swiney is not made by the impulse of the moment, but by the faithful daily living in accordance with a rule based on conviction and an ideal constantly in mind and constantly cherished."

I was scarcely eighteen when I was sent down to Killnaglass as principal of the school in that townland. Killnaglass; nowhere; County Laois. I was moving round our island. And principal! I was humbled, terrified, proud, and at a loss.

Killnaglass was a small, two-roomed school. Behind it stood the house that was called the monastery. I was met at the station by Brother Cyprian, an old Brother who took the boys up to second class. He was genial, humble, retiring and that suited me because I must have been at least forty years his junior in age and experience, yet I was to be his superior in the school. We walked together out a narrow road through a sparsely populated townland. There were furze bushes everywhere, still, in late Spring, alight with their golden blossoms. Somewhere nearby a cuckoo called; swifts and swallows flew through their network of laneways and passageways in the air, their cries sharp, high and bristling.

"Killnaglass is that kind of a place, as you'll find out, Brother, small and vast, quiet and filled with sound, Catholic and pagan, old and new." Brother Cyprian laughed, and I settled into the beauty of the day.

Brother Leo was principal in the monastery; older, too, solid as a statue's plinth, loud and full of laughter. After a good supper, a chat and a smoke, I stood outside and looked past the school into the valley, lush with growth, green, golden, the yellow-green of early shoots, the occasional households with their white-washed pleasantness, and I told myself I would be happy.

The school had great windows with long cords to open them at the top. There was an enormous teacher's desk at the top of each classroom, a little brass bell resting on it; there were cupboards crammed with the books and instruments of learning, slates, ink, marla, pencils, pens, copies ... On the wall above the fireplace a huge crucifix, on the wall at the back of the class, causing severe neck problems for the pupils, was the clock, brown, sallow-faced, with roman numerals, and a loud tick that seemed out of place in the timeless atmosphere of Killnaglass.

I had charge of the school and taught second to sixth class. I settled in with enthusiasm, the boys being simple, rough and homely, I no more than six or seven years older than some of them. I began each day with prayers, and then I read out to them a passage from their "Irish History Reader".

"The pupils," the passage went, "must be taught that Irishmen, claiming the right to make their own laws, should never rest content until their native Parliament is restored; and that Ireland looks to them, when grown to man's estate, to act the part of true men in furthering the sacred cause of nationhood."

They watched me, eager and hopeful as I had been, and I felt they were soaking in the words the way a parched earth soaks in the rain.

There was one boy, quieter, better-spoken than the others: Robert Hake, son of Major Ronald Thornton Hake, of the big house beyond Carrow Wood. Robbie was small, well-mannered and well-dressed where the others were big and gruff and dressed in tatty, patched gansies and trousers. Robbie always wore a jacket, shirt and tie; his shoes were shoes, laced and polished; the others wore boots, grey and studded, or else they thumped on the ground with naked, hardened feet. Robbie never volunteered information, always waiting to be asked and then he would answer pertly, correctly, most of the questions I put to him. When I gathered them in a circle round me near the blackboard he would hold back a little, hover in the second row, alert and willing.

There was to be an examination in religion undertaken by the parish priest at the beginning of June. Soon after that the Bishop would come, bringing Confirmation to those who had satisfied the priest they were strong and perfect Christians. I got down to the task with enthusiasm. Robbie Hake's hand was in the air.

"Robbie?" I prodded.

"Brother, I'm not to do the Confirmation."

"Why not, Robbie?"

"I'm not a Catholic, Brother. My father says I'm to miss the classes and asks if I can study something else at this time, please."

Major Thornton Hake was accepted in the world of Killnaglass. Land-holder, landlord, Protestant, he rode to hounds with the men of the Kilnagh Hunt. He stayed aloof from the people but gave employment on the estates and was reported fair, honest, not to be trifled with. The agony was the river where he kept exclusive fishing rights; and there were pheasants he bred on his estates and shooting-parties for his friends. The Major was tolerated as they tolerated weathers, as they accepted strange trees and exotic plants, as they accepted the high walls around the demesne. And the people were accepted by the Major, as he accepted the need to keep accounts, to repair walls and restock rivers.

I had hoped for the saving of Robbie's soul by gentle insistence and by example.

"No, Robbie," I said. "While you're in my school you will do what the others do. I cannot make exceptions. So, you will pay attention while we're on the Confirmation classes, I will not ask you questions and Father Quinn will excuse you from the examination. But I can't have a class set aside especially for you."

And we got down to the workings of the faith.

Robbie stood in the half-circle, his small, respectful face attentive, his hands behind his back, his head to one side. I could see he had answers to questions that the others did not have. But I did not ask him, even when the dullness of the others dragged heavily against my spirit. My consolation was in the subtlety of my subterfuge.

Next morning, after the daily prayers, and the rollcall, when I told them to pick up their "Irish History Reader" and open it at my special paragraph, "The pupils must be taught that Irishmen, claiming the right to make their own laws ... " Robbie again stood up in his desk and waited for attention.

"Robbie?"

"Brother, please, my father has asked me to beg your pardon but may I be excused from the passage from the history reader. Please."

He spoke stoutly, knowing it must cause difficulty, and I leaned towards him in sympathy. This, I knew, was a summons to the Major's presence, a peremptory demand that I explain myself, that he be given a chance to put me down and exalt his own position and his faith. A summons into the barrack-yard of the enemy.

"No, Robbie, I'm sorry, no," I answered him at once, "my answer must be the same. We cannot make rules and then break them when we feel they do not suit our purposes. You will please read from your reader, with everybody else."

During lunch break, some days later, while I sat in the other room, chatting with Brother Cyprian, there came a whooping and a cheering from the playground, so tensed with enthusiasm that I knew something special was afoot. I walked out, casually, Cyprian behind me.

At the back of the yard were the sheds, one for turf, the other euphemistically known as "the lavatories". This was a long shed with a wooden bench along its back wall, holes opening onto a drain below. It was a place ugly beyond belief, heavy in its stench, a nightmare even when the drain moved swiftly under mountain rains. In wet weather, it oozed a pestilential steam, in dry it sweated a green slime.

The boys were gathered round the one opening to the lavatory shed. They moved back when I appeared. They kept jeering and hooting, a note of ugly glee in their voices.

I glanced into the shed; Robbie Hake was hanging by his hands from one of the wooden beams, his mouth gagged with a dirty cloth, he was blindfolded and his feet were tied together with a rag. The twine holding his hands to the beam was a thin one, and would snap if the boy jerked in his efforts to escape. He was hanging directly over one of the holes in the toilet bench. He was deathly still when I arrived, turning slowly, like a hare strung up to drip away its blood. I was so horrified that I stood helpless for a moment, my whole body pounding with agony for the boy.

I called Brother Cyprian to help; swiftly we moved, Cyprian holding Robbie about the knees while I stood on the boards and snapped the twine from the roofbeam. Robbie stayed rigid in Cyprian's grip until I was able to take him under the arms. We carried him out into the fresh air and began to ease the rags and cloths that bound him. There was silence now from the blackguards in the yard. How much suppressed hatred, bitterness and hurt were stored up in the quiet houses of Killnaglass it was impossible to calculate. But this day's horror struck me a sudden blow to the stomach.

Robbie's wrists were bleeding where the twine had cut into his flesh. His body trembled like a frightened bird's, his eyes were bright and moist with horror, when he tried to speak he stammered uncontrollably. For some reason, the ugly size and angry shape of Big Con Rohan flashed before my eyes, the awful power of his small, squat penis, and I too began to shiver before the dark weathers of the human heart. I took Robbie gently by the shoulders and asked Cyprian to take him to the monastery and get him to drink a hot cup of tea. Robbie stood upright, though trembling, and began to walk slowly ahead of Cyprian, towards the monastery. I turned to face the boys.

The older, bigger ones were leering confidently as I walked through them towards the school. Several of the smaller ones, from Brother Cyprian's classes, were pale and frightened. My mind was made up. The school was a two-room school with a small porch in between where coats were hung and milk was boiled for cocoa. Two doors opened into the classrooms from the porch. I stood in the door of the school and blew my whistle. It was twenty minutes to one.

Almost at once the infant classes passed by me and into their room; the older boys came more slowly, a mixture of sullenness and smugness on their faces. I looked into the eyes of each boy as he passed and picked out four of the sixth class boys I suspected of being the sources of the crime. I said nothing as I let them pass me, almost touching my body.

When my class was in I went to the top of the room and stood before them. Without a word, and for the first time since I had come into their classroom, I opened the cupboard and selected the most wicked-looking cane I could find. The whispering and rustling in the classroom died away as I tried it out on the air, slicing it viciously down and thudding it off the folds of my soutane. Then I left the cane on my table and, still not offering them a word, left my class and went into Cyprian's room. The little boys were stunned and quiet.

"You may all go home now," I said to them, "and you will tell your parents how the children of Killnaglass have disgraced themselves. You will tell them that I am ashamed today to be an Irishman. And you can tell your parents there will be no classes in this school until the boys who have done this terrible thing apologise in public to Robbie Hake. Go, and do not come back until you know that the guilty have been punished for their sin."

Hurriedly they gathered their poor bags and copies, their pencils and enamel mugs and they went from the room. As they scurried down the path to the front gate I could hear the excited hum of their words. I stood awhile in the porch, watching them go, allowing my figure to be seen by the boys waiting in my own room, letting them stew a while longer in the juices of their apprehension.

I left the school door and the door of my classroom open, and I walked slowly back to the top of the class. I felt that the smirking and snickering had been replaced by a tangible nervousness; they sat rigid in their desks, fingers fiddling with the inkwells, fingernails picking at the wooden surface of the desks.

"Six slaps," I began, "six slaps, that's no terrible thing. The horrible crime you have done has been done by only a few. There are four perhaps, maybe more, maybe less, guilty of the crime, though each of you is guilty because you all went along with it. You have disgraced the name of Killnaglass by showing everyone you are no better than the invaders when they handed down the tortures our ancestors had to suffer. Now I am giving you a chance to redeem the honour you have lost. If those three or four boys, from our Confirmation class I have no doubt, admit their guilt, simply tell me, now, the truth, then they will receive only six slaps each, no more, they will apologise to young Robbie Hake and everything will be back to normal. Let me see, now, how truth and honour are valued, here in Killnaglass."

Though I spoke firmly I was shaking through my entire body. I stood before them, half a dozen years, scarcely more, separating me from them, yet I felt, at that moment, so much older, so much wearier. I stood, pivotal for a while in the circle of their young lives and I offered them an opportunity to seize on truth as the axle round which they could move.

There was hardly a stir among them. They gazed at the fallow fields of their desks. They glanced surreptitiously at one another.

I let a full ten minutes pass in silence. Still there was no movement towards the truth. The heavy clock ticked on, aided by the occasional creaking of a desk, the hint of birdsong from outside, and once, the distant, mocking bray of a jackass. A great despondency settled about my life.

"Alright," I said at length, "you are telling me there is no honour left in Killnaglass. I will ask each boy, one by one, if he was involved in this crime. It is your last chance to grasp honour and truth. As I ask you, you will take your bag and you will go home. If I learn the truth today, then school will be as usual tomorrow. If I do not get the truth then this school will remain shut until such time as you yourselves, or your parents, decide to restore the truth to your lives. If I do not find the truth then I will know for certain that there is no boy here worthy of being a

Christian and I will tell the Bishop that the sacrament of Confirmation is not possible in Killnaglass this year."

I brought each one from his desk to stand before me, and I asked, solemnly, the question:

"Were you involved in what was done to Robbie Hake?"

The answers came, sometimes in a strong voice, sometimes whispered, sometimes stammered; "No Brother," and each one packed his bag and headed home, full of the news from our school. Third class, fourth class, fifth. Finally, into sixth class. There were boys here even thirteen years of age, some of them as tall as me, some of them more burly. A few of these I knew, in my heart, to be guilty. Slowly I went through the class, leaving those I suspected till the end. Four big, brutish boys, eyeing me with caution and daring.

"Patrick Clane, were you involved in what was done to Robbie Hake?"

"No, Brother!" Spoken too quickly to be true.

"John James McMahon, were you involved in what was done to Robbie Hake?"

Two of them left.

"Séamus O'Máille … "

One left: Vincent Joseph Finn, son of the village butcher, thirteen, plump, red-faced, still in short pants, ungainly, every inch a bully. I left him sitting alone for a while, I put the cane back into the cupboard. I tidied the cupboard. I went out, for a moment, into the porch. I stood outside and waited. Through the bushes I could see Clane, McMahon and O'Máille, lurking, waiting. Wondering. I waited, too. Vincent Joseph Finn watched me out of the corner of his eye, his hands lost on the great desert of his desk.

Finally I came and sat in a desk beside him. I looked at him and he met my gaze a while, then dropped it, shuffled uncomfortably and, as I had hoped, began to blubber. His eyes blinked rapidly and I saw tears coming.

I had my man!

"Now, Vincent, it will be very easy indeed to end all of this nonsense. You have a great opportunity to become a man before all of them, to show them, and me, that you value truth and honesty. Robbie is a good youngster and you know that; nobody deserves the torture you were putting him through. Come on, then, let's get this over. Vincent, I tell you that only the truth is beautiful."

He opened his mouth and no words came out. He looked at me, his eyes wet, the words waiting. But he looked away again, quickly, and I had lost him. When he looked back at me I was amazed at the defiance in his face.

"The book, Brother," he said, "you read that book every morning. It says we must be Irishmen and make our own laws and when we do, or when someone else does, then you make it into a crime, Brother ... " A rush of words that slithered back into silence, words that were like stones I myself had flung high into the air and that now dropped back on my own life. I went through the ritual with him.

"Vincent Joseph Finn ... "

I asked him three times, and there times he answered, "No, Brother," until I released him and he followed the others into the early afternoon.

The empty classroom was oppressive in its silence, a beam of sunlight falling across the vacant desks, dust motes and chalk motes mingling in the air, the great green map of Ireland on the wall with the six counties coloured in a screaming orange, hanging dead and ugly, the pain high in my chest drumming at me until I had to get up and go out into the freshness of the day, to gulp in great, relieving breaths. When I had regained some composure I went back in and knelt on the rough boards of the schoolroom floor, folded my hands together and watched towards the crucifix high on the classroom wall.

DAVID

HOW STRANGE THE SOUND OF HIS VOICE WHEN IT CAME UP TO ME through the foliage of the pine-trees. Distant, from another world. Perhaps God sits like that, abstracted, turned in upon Himself, resenting the intrusion of our prayers.

I was sitting in the wind that day, high up in the tree, drowning myself in the soughing of the pine-tops, holding the rough bark of the tree, allowing my body to be cradled in the berceuse of movement, all the anguish and love and fear of life flowing with the anguish and rhythms of the tumbling world. His voice came from the needle-covered earth, reaching up to where I flew.

"Where are you?" he shouted.

Sound rises easily; but the answering call from above is muted, distant and unreal.

"Come down! just for a minute," he shouted against the foliage, and the wind, "there's just one small thing I want to say."

I clambered down, carefully, wondering. I dropped the last few feet from the bottom branches, and stood, brushing myself off. There were little gouts of pine-resin on my hands, their fragrance filling the air about us, the stickiness of the tree's life-blood making my own hands tacky and uneasy. I looked into his face. I could see he was embarrassed. I rubbed my hands against the pockets of my trousers.

"You are going to-morrow to join the Holy Ghost Fathers ... " he began, as if I didn't know that, as if I had not made that choice myself many months ago, as if the pain and enormity of it had not driven me up into the sky to breathe in the rough comfort of the air. "And I wish you every joy and every blessing, you know that."

His eyes were steady, on my face, and I looked down to the ground, to the thick carpet of brown pine-needles, those millions of individual pieces that had merged together over the years into a brown softness.

"Yes."

"Well, what I want you to know is this, that if ever, at any stage, you feel that you do not have a vocation, then you must come home to us at once, at once, do you hear? and not be afraid in any way that you're doing wrong, or letting us down, or anything like that. Do you understand?"

"Yes, I know that, but I do not intend to give up. I know this is my vocation, and I am grateful for it, I'm feeling very lonely now but still … "

Oh the pathos of human pride, the bathos of a heart that has taken up its position and feels itself unassailable!

He reached forward, put his hand on my shoulder and allowed the weight of his life to rest on me for a moment. He smiled, then shook my shoulder, gently.

"I just wanted you to be certain … " he began, then broke off.

"These trees will miss you, you know, always climbing in them, swinging like an old monkey, the trees, the branches, they'll all miss you, you know that. And listen! this will always be your place, always, if ever … "

Yes, Dad, I knew that, I knew you would miss me, and I knew that I would miss Achill, and the grove, and your own, solid presence ahead of me in my life. I knew I would feel, tomorrow, that a strong wall had been taken from in front of me, that I would be left standing, at the age of eighteen, swaying, on the edge of a precipice of my own making. Where, now, will I find a place? where, now, can I turn?

"It can be hard, sometimes, to die."

MATTHEW

ROBBIE WOULD NOT SPEAK THE NAMES OF HIS TORTURERS. THE afternoon in the monastery passed in uneasy silence. I could sense the upset in Brother Leo's life but he did not criticise me. The day sank slowly into the pool of thick mud it had created about itself. I hardly slept all night, I turned and hurt in bed, night pressing down on me with the weight of a dead animal.

Brother Cyprian and I were at the door of the school before nine next morning. Nobody came, the countryside green and alien beyond our gate, swifts and swallows slicing through the air, breezes stirring the rhododendron bushes. At ten we returned to the monastery. I sat a while in my own room, trying to read. I heard a knock on the monastery door and Brother Leo's voice talking quietly. Soon there was a tap on my door.

"Mrs Lavelle called to find out about school," Leo said. "I told her it was closed for a few days until we had a problem sorted out. Was that alright?"

"Yes, Leo, thank you. And, em, what? or, rather, how did she react?"

"She seemed a bit pleased, to me."

"Oh! and why would that be, do you think?"

"Well, the weather is up, you see, and there's the turf to be done and young Jimmy Lavelle is a fine worker ... "

After lunch I ventured out of the monastery and took the road towards the village church. I felt guilty, as if I were the one at fault. I met no-one though I saw families in the fields as I passed. I walked through the scattered houses of Killnaglass. Only a few mongrel dogs paid me heed.

The statues in the chapel irritated me. The silence within was rich with the colours of ministering angels, with the presence of God, with the hope that still hummed somewhere within me. I tried to enter into that silence but the noise of untruth coming from the statues and the gaudy Stations interrupted and disturbed me. St Joseph, a huge lily in his hand, held the child Jesus in the palm of one hand as if the baby, ugly, leering, old-man-faced, were a dream. The colours were crude and crudely daubed. Mary, her crooked eyes turned towards the ceiling, her mantle a dirty blue, chipped to show the stained white of plaster beneath, the gold of her girdle, the purple of the rosary she held in her chipped hands, all were loud and vibrating in the air. The everpresent thudding in my chest grew loud in that unholy place.

I left the chapel, blessed myself and turned back towards the village. There was a man standing before me on the road, big, red-faced, balding, his shirt-sleeves rolled up, his arms muscular, his fists big and purple. I nodded and made to pass him by. He stepped out, in my way. I noticed the dirt that made his trousers almost rigid in their folds, the great boots he wore, wildly laced, without stockings.

"Would you be Brother Gonzalez, now?" he demanded, his voice belying the bulk of his body, a voice sharp and musical.

"Yes, indeed, I'm Brother Gonzalez. And I'm happy to make your acquaintance. Who might I have here?"

"I might be Bartholomew Finn, butcher, so I might, and Vincent Joseph Finn might be my boy now, so he might, an' all."

Spoken with slowness in which a restrained violence

was simmering.

"Oh, Mr Finn, I'm glad to meet you," and I stretched out my hand towards him. He ignored it, and I let my hand drop back to my side, where it hung, trembling and unsure.

"You accused my lad of attacking that young Hake fellow, now, so I've been hearing?" Put as a question, I gathered, a question, asked quietly.

"No indeed, Mr Finn, I merely attempted to discover which boys tried to do immense harm to a young boy guilty of nothing but of being different from them."

"Oh, different he is alright, I grant you that. But, as I hear it, you kept my lad till last and told him to own up to it and he didn't do nothin', as I'm pretty damn sure now he didn't!" Put this time, not as a question, but an accusation.

"Please believe me, Mr Finn, I never ... "

"Now, my lad don't tell lies, that you can believe, 'cos if he did I swear I'd slice his fat arse into rashers with my belt so I would, and have done so before. And for that he's sent home from school, the whole school's closed, from what I hear." Put as a threat, this time, the purple fists bunched, the great body squat, like a wall, before me.

"I assure you, Mr Finn, there is no cause for worry. perhaps if I could speak with Vincent, in your presence ... ?"

"No call, no call, I have him out beyond now in the meadows where he'll prove himself useful for a day or two. But he's to be confirmed in this here Chapel at the end of the month, and he'll be leavin' school come July and I won't have this broken down because a young whippersnapper just out of short pants doesn't know his arse-hole from a boghole. And I want my Vincent back in school by the day after tomorrow or Batty Finn will be askin' why. Good day to you now. You can be gettin' back to your prayers ... "

He turned from me and carried his load of flesh back

into the village. Slowly I put my black hat on my head. I realised I had been holding myself stiff before an anticipated physical onslaught. As I breathed out, I felt my whole body fall weak and I had to lean against a fencing post until some strength returned.

At nine fifteen next morning several boys turned up at school, Vincent Finn was not among them. Brother Cyprian and I allowed them into the classrooms where they chattered until nine thirty. Then I stood before my group and again asked that those involved step forward. I was greeted now with titters. One of the boys – I was so shaken that I seemed to be seeing him through a haze – said, "I thought Batty Finn had cleared that up, Brother?" There was a titter from the class. I dismissed them, angrily, shouting at them, shouting for lack of confidence in what I was about.

We returned to the monastery and I knelt in my room to pray for guidance. I was weak, tired, dispirited. I knelt at the side of the bed and felt the pain in my chest pulse and throb.

I was jerked violently to my feet by the sound of glass being shattered. Then the window in my room was smashed and a large stone crashed onto the floor beside the bed. I rushed outside but there was no sign of anyone, the rhododendron woods around the monastery were dense and extensive. Every window along the front of the building was smashed, the coloured glass frames around and above the front door were shattered, there was blood on my hands and I realised I had picked up an icicle of glass from the floor and was holding it clenched in my fist.

Brother Cyprian was in tears, sitting in the kitchen, head buried in his hands. Leo was putting on his coat. He barely glanced at me, muttered he was going to cycle out to see Canon Horan, and then the guards.

"You must do something, Brother Blake, you must

do something ... "

I walked out from Killnaglass along by the high, gracefully curving wall of the Hake Estate. Here the trees leaned out over the walls, beech and oak and ash. The gateway had two aristocratic pillars, with stone eagles rampant on top, beaks wide and cruel. I walked up the gravel driveway that twisted and turned like a snake; on either side rich bushes of hydrangea and semi-exotic plants whose names I did not know; there was a deep-green laurel hedgerow, and beyond, with clumps of majestic trees – chestnut, elm, pine – the grazing-lands and meadows of the estate. I was walking into the arms of the enemy.

After a half-mile or so the driveway opened onto a large, empty space; straight ahead was the house, big, pillared, white, high windows suggestive of luxury within, the house itself, in its squat power, forbidding entry by any but the confident, the great, the conqueror. Immediately to my right was a high brick wall with a door standing open; through it I glimpsed an orchard. A great black Labrador came pouncing and barking through that door. I bent towards it, my hands eager to touch and fondle it, in its wondrous animal sheen, its innocence and truth. We were immediate companions, that animal and I, both in black, one more shabby, both servants, suitors to the rich and great.

I heard a shout: – "Landor! Landor!" – angry and authoritative, from somewhere behind that orchard wall. The dog nuzzling against my leg, I made my way towards the door. Major Hake came striding through fine apple-trees towards me. He carried a rifle, breached, under his right arm. He was a small man, thin and balding, where I had expected a large-sized bully. Only his face, stern and certain, placed him apart, and the fine set of his riding-clothes, dark green jacket, jodhpurs, boots. Wisps of a straw-coloured hair were blowing everywhichway about the pink baldness of his head; his left hand swept them impatiently back. His eyes were narrowed, watchful; his ferret face ended in a small, straw-coloured goatee beard.

He called again:

"Here, Landor! come, come boy, come boy, heel!"

The dog ran to its master who turned quickly from me and began to walk back the way he had come. But he spoke over his shoulder, flinging the words in my direction.

"Brother Gonzalez, I'll wager. Come, boy, come, I'm down here by the rabbit-run. Come and make your speech."

He strode quickly through the orchard and I followed, lost to know how to deal with him. But he paid more attention to his poet-dog than to me, muttering to him, patting his head; I followed, dog-at-the-heel, reluctant.

We came out through the trees into a yard with a long patch of earth, about one hundred yards in length, fenced in to make a run some three feet wide. On each side were trees and shrubbery; the run ended with a wire fencing and beyond that rich meadowland. At the near end, among sheds and stables, I saw a cage filled with hares and rabbits. They cowered and nibbled, twenty to thirty of them, eyes wide, ears pressed back along their bodies. I understood the game at once, and my stomach heaved against it.

The Major had stopped at the tightly-meshed wicket gate at this end of the run. There was a cartridge-belt hanging from the gate. He took two cartridges and loaded the gun. The dog lay down at his feet, tail wagging expectantly.

"You're only a boy. I'm surprised. I'm surprised."

"Major, I've come to see if ... "

"Yes yes yes, you hope young Robbie will get you out

of your difficulty. You want names. I've been expecting that. That crumbling before the squalid bunch of village idiots. But he won't give you names, no sir! and if he does I'll tie him to this gate and whip him roundly. Don't hold with snitching. No sir, no sir. You Irish have got to get yourselves straightened out now, all by yourselves."

He glanced at me as he said this and he saw me flush with resentment at all the history and implications in his words. He laughed, an ugly, confident laugh. Then he opened the wicket gate, lifted a low latch in the cage and hauled a rabbit out by the neck. He flung the animal far down the run and dropped the hatch back on the cage. The rabbit gathered itself together, stunned, and did not move.

"Blasted good-for-nothing beast! Now, Landor, now!"

He held the dog by its collar; it barked furiously towards the cowering creature on the run. The rabbit stirred fearfully on its awful pathway and began to move, slowly and hesitantly, along the clay. The Major closed over the wicket gate, leaned on it and put the gun to his shoulder. He fired. I saw the earth explode inches from the rabbit's tail and suddenly the creature bolted in panic down the runway.

The Major waited. The rabbit neared the fence at the end of the run.

"One for sorrow," the Major muttered and fired again.

"Two for joy!" he said as the rabbit crumpled into death, its broken body rolling over into a humiliating ugliness. Its hind legs kicked for a moment. Then it was still. The Major opened the gate and Landor bounded along the run, took the rabbit in its mouth and fetched it back to the Major's feet.

"One more," I think, the Major grunted, pleased with himself, "one more, for the monastery table."

He bent to lift the latch again, then stopped and stood

to glance at me.

"Do you shoot, boy?"

"Yes, yes, I shoot, though it's been a while ... "

"Of course, of course, don't all you Irish shoot! How could I forget; you shoot the English from behind bushes, and then you shoot each other from behind the same bushes!" and he laughed his ugly laughter tight with venom.

I restrained myself with difficulty, the pain in my chest was causing me agony.

"Right! a hare; shoot him and bring him home to grace your table!"

He had loaded the gun once more; he thrust it into my hands. It was magnificent in its weight and balance, the stock felt like velvet to my hands, the barrel long and delicate, the double trigger new to me and feverishly exciting.

"Shoots straight and true, boy. First shot to scare 'em down the run. Second when you think fit – but make some sport of it, let the creature have a chance!"

He heaved out a hare, big and strong and elegant and he flung it vigorously out onto the run. While the hare picked itself back into its senses the Major closed the gate and thrust me forward. I leaned the barrel on the top bar of the gate and aimed. Oh! it was a good feeling, the power and certainty of that weapon in my hands! The pain seemed to have vanished from my chest and that old feeling of exhilaration, as if the world were in my control, came flooding back to me.

"One for sorrow ... " murmured the voice at my shoulder.

I touched the first trigger and blasted a hole less than an inch from the tail of the hare.

"Fine shot, Sir!" came the voice, touched with genuine admiration. "Right, now. Wait! Yahoooo!"

The startled hare had leaped forward, then paused again. The Major's shout sent it whopping away down the path and I aimed again, remembering my father's words, "when you aim ... the trigger-touch ... the vulnerable spot ... the love ... " I would show this thin bully how I could shoot. I touched the second trigger; the hare was less than twenty yards from the fence; I could so easily have brought it down but something gave inside me, images surfaced, soldiers in the yard at home shooting at hens, the heron blown in misery out of the sky ... I shot over the ears of the hare, the bullet vanishing into distance beyond the meadow. The creature disappeared into the long grasses beyond the fence.

I sensed the Major was aware of what I had done and he was both amused and annoyed. He took the gun back from me and began to reload.

"Weakness of will, boy, I'm afraid, no guts for the kill. Like that Eamon de Valera of yours. No guts, like Collins, to stay the course."

It was calculated, of course, and the jab hurt, and he knew it. Before I could respond he reached into the game-bag and drew out a hen-pheasant, its lovely pride destroyed.

"Here, boy," he reached it towards me, "take it home as consolation. The meat of a bird, you know, especially of a hen, is less of a spur to the sexual appetites than the demanding flesh of an animal."

I was stung to respond.

"You, sir, are as cruel to your fellow human beings as you are to the most helpless of animals."

"You, boy, in your black disguise and your chants and rituals, you are incapable of running a school! You're a baby, a baby at a man's task. Take them, before they master you, cane them, cane them till they beg for mercy, till they beg you to listen to their confessions. Guts, boy, you lack guts!"

At that moment Robbie came round the angle of the outhouses leading a big horse by its bridle. I knew my errand to this house would be in vain; how could I expect a boy to report on his fellows even though they had treated him so badly? He would not ever recover from such betrayal, either in his own mind or before his peers.

"Ah ha!" grunted the Major with satisfaction. "My own Champion. The horse, I mean, boy, not Robbie ... " and he laughed his dirty, slug-fat laugh. As boy and horse approached, the Major turned on me again.

"On your own head this foolishness that almost tossed my boy into the shit! Your stupid rigmarole about nationhood, your native Parliament, your Republic! You haven't the guts for nationhood, not one of you!"

"De Valera is standing true to lead us!" I spoke it loudly, out of my pain and discomfiture.

"Hah!" came the grunt, "that gas-bag! He has betrayed your cause, boy, your poor, pathetic effort at a nation!"

Robbie had come up. He looked strong and bright and I caught a gleam of pleasure in his eyes as he greeted me.

"Hello, Brother Gonzalez. You're welcome."

"Thank you, Robbie," I murmured, feeling a surge of gratitude towards his innocence. But the Major had thrust the gun into my hands, he was buckling on the heavy cartridge-belt. Then he swung himself up into the saddle.

"Don't you know your de Valera has abandoned Sinn Féin?" He mocked me from his position high above.

"What do you mean?"

"He has grown tired of standing like a clown outside the doors to your poor Dáil and now he wants to get a foot inside. Sinn Féin won't have it, they want to fight with shadows, like the rest of you. So now de Valera won't have Sinn Féin. There are real shadows to fight inside your Dáil, he says. And Sinn Féin won't have him. You fight amongst yourselves again, no guts, boy, no guts for the real battles."

This was terrible news to me.

"But he cannot enter the Dáil," I stuttered, "he can never take the oath of allegiance to an English monarch!"

"Ha! you Irish are experts at just one thing, and that is subterfuge!" the Major laughed, settling himself in his saddle, sneering down at me. "He has resigned Sinn Féin and taken half the sodden fools along with him. And he has formed another party, Fianna Fáil or some such childish prankster name, and has announced his intention of taking his gang of fools into your parliament."

He was enjoying the dismay that must have been obvious throughout my whole body.

"But," I stammered, "the oath, the oath … "

"Words, boy, words, he says, just words, an empty formula he says, and he will take the oath, he says, but will not mean it! Jesuit! Liar! Fool! What is truth, Gonzalez, I ask you, what is truth?" He was laughing out loud as my whole soul shrank at the overwhelming sense of betrayal I felt at that moment.

"Where is your nation now, Gonzalez? where is your republic? founded on grace and truth! Psah! Founded on lies, hypocrisy, cowardice! My gun, boy, hand me up my gun!"

I was trembling with anger and frustration, with humiliation before this age-old enemy, this bully looking down at me. I longed, at that moment, to be back with my father at the Glenshale Pass, to be in the house with the Tans, and I would assault them, take them in the violence of my passion and kill them! I moved towards the Major and for one long, bewildering moment I felt that I was going to raise his own gun against him and aim, lovingly, truly, at the spot in the centre of his forehead, the entry point into the dark boghole of his soul. It was a vivid moment, a star on the rim of my circle, but it passed, quickly, into dullness. I believe he was disappointed as I turned the rifle butt towards him.

"Guts, Gonzalez, find them, find them quickly and tear those blackguards from the company of my son!"

"Yes," I shouted, "the way de Valera will yet tear your privileged monsters from the suffering flesh of our country. Leeches you are, leeches, sucking the blood of a country that has put up with your ugliness for too long!"

I was beneath him then, he had the rifle, he swung it out at me with a sudden viciousness. I heard him scream some obscenity, the barrel of the gun caught me hard in the jaw and I fell backward, the world becoming a fireball of scarlet before my eyes; my chest roared in agony, my mind lost all words and thoughts into a great swirling mass of darkness.

DAVID

HE BROUGHT ME, ONE DAY, OUT THE BACK DOOR OF THE HOUSE
and up to the bog fields behind our meadows. Here the
world was big, there was a lake, bogland stretched away
into the flanks of the mountain. To right and left only a
few scarecrow furze bushes, heather-covered hillocks, bog-
oak roots, the winds; prehistoric landscape, filled with non-
life.

He told me to wait by the last gate. Then he walked
about a hundred yards in the direction of the lake. There
was a fence-post there, fencing nothing in from nothing.
Standing alone. A spine. He had our dog's old enamel plate
with him, a hammer, a nail. He fixed the plate to the top of
the post so that it showed its off-white face in my direction.
The backdrop only the lake and the barren brown hills.

I rested the point twenty-two on one of the bars of the
gate. He showed me how to load it. I loved the stumpy
feel of the big, red cartridge, like a large lump of crayon,
and I loved how it eased itself into the breach. Then he
showed me how to rest the stock in against my shoulder,
how to close one eye and focus through the little gap,
gathering the point of the barrel through that gap and onto
the target. How to hold it still. How to try and hold myself
still. To be steady.

He stood at my right shoulder. As he spoke I could feel
his breath against the side of my head. He had his arms
about me, his body leaning on mine as he tried to line up
my sights, his left hand holding my left arm, his right hand

guiding my right hand to the trigger.

"When you aim," he said, "try and become your target. Try and get to know it, its meaning, its presence, its weight. Try to feel how it thinks, how it suffers. Take it in, be in love with it for just this moment. Then you must know where it hurts the most, where it is weakest, imagine its death-wound already there, where it is, the open sore, and then you touch that sore, gently, with compassion, and that is the trigger touch, gentle, gentle, a squeezing, a caress. Touch the trigger with sympathy, with sorrow even, but above all, with love."

I didn't understand a word of what he was saying. What I saw before me was an off-white enamel plate. But I was excited by the simplicity of it all. I had seen him bring birds down out of the sky, I had seen him come home with rabbits, hares, wild geese … I pulled the trigger. There was a recoil and I knew I hadn't got my shoulder firmly enough against the stock. The gun resounded, a sharp, loud crack that went off over the gorse and lake like a snipe.

"Well," he said, "that's one lucky plate! To be standing at that post might be the safest place in Achill. We'll have to try again. Be gentle. Remember, caress the target. Put your shoulder more definitely against the gun. Pull the trigger slowly, like I told you … "

I fired six times, trying to follow his directions. Then I left down the gun and we walked together to see what damage I had done to the enamel plate. The large, white body of the dish was untouched.

"Maybe the bullets passed through so fast they left no mark behind them," he laughed.

I was silent.

"We'll try it another day," he said. "Maybe you're too young yet to take so much weight on your shoulders. The gun. It's a serious business, you know."

He pulled the plate and nail out of the post and sent it twirling, a small space-ship, into the emptiness of the bog.

Once before he vanished out of our lives. For what? Two weeks, was it, three weeks? Longer? It seemed much longer. I was too young to see behind the mystery of his absence. Like a great hole in my life, a silence swelling until I thought it would burst, a foreign language offered in answer to my questions. I did not know where to turn.

We were driven by a neighbour to the hospital at last, and I could feel the constraint as he rose to meet us from a bench at the end of a great hallway. His face, badly bruised and cut in places, as if he'd been in a terrible fight, as if he'd had an accident. And his arm, too, bandaged. A mystery to me. Still.

The way he ignored me then to move quickly to my mother, to kiss her lightly on the forehead, the way both he and she chattered, too noisily, about silly things and I just hung there, outside them, alone. Until he caught me up, lifted me high and hugged me ...

Where had he been? And what had happened that he should abandon me like that?

I used to walk out the road to meet him. He would finish work at three o'clock, he would have to stay back sometimes to clear things up, put away books and copies and things, lock up the school, then drive the five miles home. On dry evenings I went to meet him, seeing how far I could get before he'd come along. Two miles, three, even four.

Sometimes I'd just sit on the parapet of the bridge over Stoney River, three miles along the road, dangle my legs over the edge, watch the golden brown water move cleanly and rapidly over the stones below, imagine the small golden eels and watch for the dark shadow of a trout.

He loved that part of the river, too, and he'd stop, turn off the engine, come and lean over the parapet with me for a while, together we'd relish the lovely whisperful quality of the river's movement, and he breathed out all the must of his day, the dust and paper and ink and school-smells, and breathed in the sweet existence of the mountainside and this clear vein of its life that ran down through heather and bogbanks, passed under our road, carried onwards to the sea. Until at last he'd touch me gently on the shoulder and say, "Right, then, riverboy, let's get back to the world."

On that particular day I reached the bridge with a certain sense of misgiving. Mother had been unusually quiet and abstracted and I slipped out without saying anything to her. I started out later than usual, I was sure I wouldn't get anywhere near the bridge before he came. But I reached the bridge, climbed onto the wall and waited. The road stretched emptily away, there was no sound but the wind moving through the telephone wires, an occasional meadow pipit chirping in the heathers, the steady rumour of the river. Soon a donkey and cart came clattering down a stone track from the mountain, a man sitting sideways on the shaft, the creaking loud on the hard ruts of the track.

Its slow coming seemed to emphasise the emptiness. As the cart trundled onto the road and the iron rims of the wheels made a different, humming sound on the tarmacadam, the man called out something and raised his stick in salute. I smiled and swung my legs more rapidly. I looked out along the road, I stood up on the parapet of the bridge; there was no sign. The cart bundled itself away into silence; there was the first hint of the day darkening; I felt betrayed, I was resentful for the first time as if something had fallen away between us. I jumped down from the bridge and began the long, tedious trudge towards home.

He did not come home at all that evening. Mother was

as restless as I was, coming and going to the window, looking out, sending me to the top of the road to gaze out over the island before it got too dark.

"Any sign?"

"No, no sign."

And she rubbed her hands against her dress and said,

"If he's not back by eight he'll probably be away for a few days. Say a prayer that everything goes all right."

FOUR

MATTHEW

I BELIEVE MAJOR HAKE WOULD NOT HAVE CARED IF HE HAD KILLED
me! He had me carried on a cart to the monastery where
the Provincial, Brother Celestine, had arrived to censure
me. I was hurt, but not seriously. More importantly, my
nerves, they say, had broken under the strain.

They brought me to St Martin's Hospital in the city. An
asylum, a lunatic asylum, though they would not call it
that. There was something about the dark, louring aspect
of the building that made me go into a frenzy of
speculation about the jackdaws and starlings squabbling
over the gables and the turrets; they were all Christian
Brothers, the place was Hell and they its keepers. Abandon
hope, all ye ...

Brother Celestine and Brother Cyprian came with me,
on the train, Cyprian to keep me calm and Celestine to sign
whatever papers were necessary. Perhaps, at some stage,
every life must go down into the darkness of the pit and
begin a long painful circling to find new light. Mine was no
dark night of the soul. It was a fall out of light and the
possibility of light into a dimness where only distorting

mirrors hung, and shifted and moved with my every shift and move.

I was undressed by two enormous men dressed all in white. They were grubs, ugly and squat and powerful. I laughed and cried at them, flailing my arms and legs like a baby. Big Con Rohan. Tans. The white that they wore was not a real white, it was off-white, threatening, and the texture of their skin was hard, like leather.

They carried me between them down a long corridor, through a door one of them unlocked, down a steeply spiralling staircase, down, always down, through another door and along a dark and eerily silent corridor. I can clearly remember it, doors, like cell doors, on either side, no windows, no pictures on the walls, no carpet on the stone floor, only one pale, naked bulb lit half-way down the corridor. They unlocked a door and bundled me inside. And I began the terrible ascent back towards the light.

I was in a hole under the earth, my arms tied tightly in front of me in a stiff, grey vest. There were no furnishings in the cell and the only light came through a tiny window at least nine feet above me in the wall, bars on the inside, no way to get to the grime-covered almost opaque glass of that window. Here I screamed myself to a frenzy, rushing at walls and doors in an effort to escape the phosphorescent fires in my head. Until I fell on the single mattress laid on the floor and passed into the relief of unconsciousness. Settling into my coffin. Underground, far underground.

Time passed, I have no idea how long I spent down there. Through the window there was no blue sky, only what looked like the black face of a stone wall. My rushes grew less frenzied, my screams less piercing and less frequent, and the long, high-pitched yelling in my head settled down to a low-pitched wail. At times I felt as if my whole being, body and soul, must burst apart the way a small body, blasted by gunshot, will burst into an obscene mess.

Exhausted, I sat against the wall, my hands aching in their permanent position across my chest, my head fallen forward like a dying plant, the reek of my own filth rising to assail me. It was at this stage a first, small awareness began to come back to me. I noticed a tiny hatch high in the door; it was opened and there was space for two eyes to take me in. At first I merely became aware of the fact, it was a hint of light from the world. I dropped my head again.

After that – that evening? or a week later? – my two grub-devils were feeding me when a sudden, deep revulsion took me for the lukewarm, bland and porridge-textured mush they were spooning into me. I allowed my mouth to be crammed full of the stuff and then I spat it straight back into the face of one of my tormentors. He bunched his fist and smashed it hard into my stomach. I doubled up at the ferocity of the blow but he grabbed me by the hair of my head, held me upright and slapped me hard, right cheek, left cheek, again, again, until I went limp in his hand and he let me crumple down on the floor before him. I vomited at his feet and then I fell forward onto my sickness and passed away again into unconsciousness.

When I came back into the world I was more alert than I had been for a long time. I squirmed, a slug, to the wall, rolled myself over and sat for a while, my back against the stones, then stood, by pushing my body upwards against the wall. The throbbing pain in my chest was almost unbearable, a loud, harsh thumping within me. I began to pace the cell, slowly, moving in an anti-clockwise direction, following a path that kept my right shoulder almost constantly in touch with the wall and brushing the small hatch in the door as I passed it by. Round and round, against the run of time, against the circle. Round and round, counting. The eyes that watched me were a very bright shade of blue, almost grey, big eyes, following my every move.

At last, rudely awakened from a long, relieving sleep, I found myself lifted and carried bodily by my two devils out of that pit of slime and back along the dim, grey corridor. I was dragged and carried up the stone steps we had descended centuries before. But not the whole way up. Another door was unlocked and I was brought along a shorter corridor, low-ceilinged, more brightly-lit than the one below. Outside one door was a wooden bench; my keepers sat me on this. I slumped back at once, exhausted by my efforts. The man who had punched and slapped me ruffled my hair, very gently, and I looked up at him in astonishment. He winked.

"Good luck, Matt!" he said, "you'll be fine. They'll get you all cleaned up in there."

I was taken into another room where they took off my strait-jacket and my vest, my trousers and underpants. I stood, a wretched, shit-soiled naked animal, forked, broken, my legs too weak to hold me. I fell onto the floor and tried to creep along on my belly. The floor was cold, I left a stain after me. I was lifted into a bath where the water was hot and lovely; they let me luxuriate in it for a time while I tried to bring some strength back into my arms. I fell asleep again and only woke when they began to pour water over me and scrub my head with a sharp-smelling liquid.

They lifted me out, then, and began to towel me dry, and I could see a great ugly rash about my stomach and down around my thighs. My penis hung tiny and lost in its little hide of hair. They shaved me, too, although my eyes kept closing and my head lolled. Finally they got me into a pair of coarse, blue-and-white-striped pyjamas and handed me over to female nurses, great white butterflies. I was too tired to speak; they held me by the arms and brought me into a small dormitory. I was asleep almost before the back of my head touched the pillow.

I slept, for how long I do not know, surfacing from that deep, black sleep now and then to be nourished and cleansed and sliding back again, without will, or intelligence, or sensual delight. Afloat and drifting on sluggish, brimful, torpid waters, on a river whose banks were warm mud, whose waters were deep and scarcely stirring.

I found myself hoisted to my feet out of the lovely fug of absence. Two nurses took me into a room where there was a high bed in the centre, bright lights from somewhere focusing on it, three attendants moving about the head of the bed. The nurses helped me up on it; it was hard, without a mattress and they strapped my hands to the sides of the bed. One of the nurses began to soothe my brows with her fingers, it was gentle, a summer breeze out of a beautiful, clear sky, she whispered to me and urged my head down onto the hard, white pillow. I felt my feet being fastened.

I looked up into the nurse's face. Her eyes were a light brown, lake water at the edges when it laps in sunshine; I could see small strands of black hair from under the white cap she was wearing; her face was pretty, softly freckled. I tried to smile at her; she was the first beautiful creature I had seen for so long and her soft hands, her quietly-breathed words, were soothing. Perhaps I smiled, because her face seemed to shiver a little, like a lake surface touched by some movement underneath, and I fancied tears were hovering at the very edges of her eyes.

Other hands were working at my brow and around the side of my head, over my ears. I ignored them. And then, a big man with eyes I recognised at once – eyes of a very light shade of blue, almost grey, big eyes, alluring – was talking at me, pushing something between my teeth, his long, ugly fingers blotched with tiny, yellow hairs, telling me to keep my teeth clenched on it, a hard, leathery texture to it, tasteless, and I held it, and I wondered. My lake-eyed nurse touched me again with the tips of her fingers; it was almost a kiss, almost a blessing. Then she stepped back and I felt alone, abandoned, lost.

When I was young I remember cockroaches creeping out onto the warm hearth in the house in Drumdouglas. I picked them up, at times, between the far-off ends of a tongs and dropped them into the crimson heart of the fire. There was a sudden, sizzling sound and the small shout of a yellow flame.

What happened to me, there on that bed, must have been a little like that instant, overwhelming, swallowing by the fire; I recall, and shudder to recall, the way the electricity took my whole body, every cell and member and finest bone of it, and seared it through with living flame. I could count my bones, I could name and identify, through its pain, every cell and artery and vein. I could see inside my own brain, like a house whose interior timbers, walls and frame were alight with a crimson flame. After that first, intolerable, instant, I remember my body jerking as if it did not belong any more to the brain that had become a boiling soup. I chomped down hard on the leather bone between my teeth and my jaws, too, ached for days.

I came to in a small room, flowers on my bedside table, a large window, the top quarter open, and white curtains billowing gently. I woke with a sense of fear as if the whole world I lived in were waiting to attack me. There was a constant, searing pain inside my head. I was, for several days, somebody other than Matthew Blake, other than Gonzalez, I had no memory whatever of who I was, or where I was, or why. I was a body pierced through with pain, unable to speak, unable to recall anything to my mind.

Nurse Sylvia Doran, she of the lake-soft eyes, told me, when I came back into the ordinary, bright fields of living, that all I murmured of intelligibility in those times was my father's name and the name of Eamon de Valera. Something, too, she thought, about fish, hake, she thought, and something about hares? She came often into my room with its ugly brown walls and spartan furnishings. She sat with me, when she could, she said I looked so young, so vulnerable, so hurt.

I was now on the first floor of St Martin's and I could sit in the alcove of my window and look out on a manicured lawn with a pebbled, rose-bordered walk. Gradually my senses began to ease and my memory return though for some time only the remoter things of my life settled back, like swallows, into their places.

One afternoon, after I had lain dozing for a time, I opened my eyes and Sylvia was in the room, humming softly to herself, her back to me. I did not stir. I grew aware of the beauty of her body. She was young, twenty-one or two, and her body was beautifully developed. The shape of her buttocks was emphasised through the tight white uniform she wore and once, as I watched, she raised the skirt high along her thigh and began to rub her flesh gently, above the spot where her dark nylon stockings were fastened by a small device. I gazed, stunned, and aroused.

Soon she was bending over me, gently bringing me awake; fussing; I had to take tablets, would I sit up a little, please Matthew, there's a good man. My eyes still half-shut, half-open, I watched her lean over me and I could see the immaculate flesh of her neck and the valley between her full breasts. I felt the stirring of a new creation within me and with it a flurry of guilt. Our eyes met and held for a moment, she looked into me as if she could see right through my brain and down into my crotch.

She smiled at me, brightly. "I'd say we're beginning to come round at last, young man! You've been going the long way round now, haven't you?"

She took my hand and held it gently against her breast, the back of my wrist sensing the wonder of her beyond the soft white stuff of her blouse. Then she was busy again, efficient and bustling and impersonal.

It was late August before I reached St Judith's ward on the fourth floor. I was dressed again in the Christian Brother suit and half-collar. There was a sun-room, "Capri" we called it, at the very end of the ward, a conservatory high above the grounds, rich with geraniums and cacti. This was Paradise, the promised land. It was a pleasure to sit here in the evenings, to smoke, to reflect on the possibilities of returning to the world.

Once Father came from Drumdouglas to see me. I was almost whole again though he told me I was a ghost. I was embarrassed before him. The word "mad" was the word the neighbours would use, "nerves" before him ... He was embarrassed, too, telling me I would be welcome to come home, nothing would be held against me, he was sure, in time ...

We talked of Ireland, of the task ahead, of building a new country. He told me of his time in jail, the hunger, the despair. About de Valera he was reticent, telling me how close he had come to the man, that it was impossible he could betray everything we had suffered for, it was impossible he could take the oath of allegiance and enter the Dáil, that Fianna Fáil would find another way to maintain the truth by which we live, or how could anyone ever take for true any statement that any of them would ever make again.

Several times Sylvia Doran came to see me. She was as beautiful to me as ever, more distant now, hesitant before my dark clothes. A reticence grew between us, a glass wall. A dull ache of loneliness replaced the furnace of pain I had been living with. When I saw her for the last time, my small brown suit-case tied with string in my hands, the daws and starlings loud as ever above the great portal of St Martin's, we shook hands shyly to say goodbye, our eyes scarcely brushed against each other, like thoughts clenched tight in their own constricting smallness amidst the whirlpooling history of the human heart.

They sent me north then, to Glenbeg, and I could gaze out into the illimitable distances of the universe. Brother Ambrose Mulcahy drove me from the station in Derry. Ambrose was as jovial as his name, round-faced, flaxen-haired, pocked and pitted in his face as if the years of his laughter had knocked humps and hollows into his flesh. The car, noisy and cold, took two hours to negotiate the distance, Ambrose talking and joking all the way, taking as much of the roughly-surfaced road as he wished. He was big, plump, the back of his wrists covered with a flaxen down.

"You can smell the sea from here, and you can hear it, too," Ambrose boomed at me, as he stretched himself, standing outside the car; "on wild days you can touch it, and taste it, carried on the winds from Iceland," and he laughed his big belly-laugh.

"You'll like it here, Gonzalez, there's a nice, quiet sandy cove over in Doonliggery Bay where you can piss away on the sand to your heart's content, and nobody will ever be the wiser. Does a man good, you know, to piss in the open air every now and then!"

The monastery was a big one, sheltered by enormous hedgerows of fuchsia; there was a grand entrance, a porchway and rooms as great as those that must exist in Hake House. On the left of the little pathway to the door was a small graveyard, the graves simple sheets of white pebbles, a tiny iron cross over each with the monk's name, his date of birth, his date of death. Over three sides of the graveyard leaned the high branches of an old sycamore, the leaves already falling, and at the top end a high white Calvary in an archway, trailing pink roses that framed it all round. I pictured a small cross raised here, my name upon it. The dream of peace began to soothe me. Rooks were loud in the trees and I could hear the cries of gulls, faintly, from the distance. There was a long low oratory Ambrose showed me, separate prie-dieus for each monk, windows of honeyed glass, a floor polished to breathlessness. We knelt, and prayed awhile, and I felt at home again, almost at peace.

I took the monastery bike, a glorious High Nelly, as often as I could and cycled over the hill, down through Lacken valley, out along the coast road, towards the Head. There was a church, Our Lady Queen of the Sea, with one enormous stained glass window picturing the Virgin, her arms spread wide in protection; through two panes under her feet you could see far out over the ocean. I sat there often, dreaming, listening to the winds howl around the angles of the building, hearing the soft echo of the waves breaking down at the Head, knowing such peace and quiet inside that I could have been a candle burning before the Sacred Heart.

Once we sat, Ambrose and I, on the end of the pier, seaweed flopping with the swell and fall-away of the tide below. Ambrose had his Franciscan sandals on, his feet, for a man so walled and rounded, were pert, delicate and white.

"I get this pain, Ambrose," I told him, "here in my chest where the Tan clobbered me. I think I can tell when it's going to rain from the pangs. I'm sure it's going to be with me all my life. And do you know? when I begin to fret again in my mind, like the beginnings of my trouble in Killnaglass, it starts to pound and I even think I can hear it, like a stallion galloping towards me across fields."

Ambrose put the palms of his hands under his great thighs and kicked his legs slowly against the pier under him.

"That's a gift of God, Gonzalez, a warning maybe that He's giving you to gather yourself back into His peace."

"You know, Ambrose, I envy you your faith. I keep praying and praying to God but the nights drag on, empty black tunnels leading only downwards into darkness."

"We all get periods like that, Gonzalez. God doesn't want us to come to Him without being aware of the value of what we're giving up. And look at the mind, man, the human mind. My head, now, it's big, big and round as a football, and I'm not the brightest man that ever walked behind Aristotle and Thomas Aquinas, but sometimes, when I'm before the blackboard and doing sums with the boys, or maybe talking away in Irish, or back in the time of Brian Boru, I have to stop myself and think, isn't it a mighty wonder now the amount of stuff stored away in one round head, ready to be called up at will, and isn't that some sort of image of what God must be, everybody's most secret thought known to Him at all times, and over all of time! Go on, man, sure the world's a wonder!"

I threw my doubts and questions into Brother Ambrose's ample lap and he took them, sucked them like sweets and found some answer. Whenever we touched on something he could not understand, he would say:

"We'll have to leave that one for the heavyweights. The Jesuits will have that one sorted out. Aren't we only the boys who do the ploughing and raking in our tiny little patches of fields, and we just can't see the whole country and how it looks. Best we get on with planting our seeds anyway, knowing if we do all as we're supposed to, the fields will green over beautifully."

"Wouldn't I love to have your calm conviction!"

He chuckled.

"Nobody knows the heart of any man, Gonzalez, maybe even God doesn't have it all clear before Him. But you're young, Gonzalez, wait until you're my age and you'll have seen so many wonders in your own back yard you'll think the place is crawling with angels and archangels."

The early days of August, after I had spent a year in the monastery, were benign and still. A sweet year. Apples swelling on the trees. The air filled with a sense of repletion as if the season were breathing deeply after its labours of growth, pausing now to preen and stretch itself before the labours of the harvest. Mackerel streaming by out in the bay. I felt physically strong, my body at peace, my mind eased, quiet in its own preserve.

I sat on the white garden seat in front of the monastery. Around me the lupins were tall, bees active about them. The trees around the graveyard scarcely moved. I watched a flycatcher flit from the branch of an elm, flick out and back, quick as an elastic band. It was mid-morning; time of peace; time when the Virgin was startled out of her stillness by the words of a passionate angel. I heard the sound of the old car long before it came around the side of the monastery and drew up before the gate. Brother Provincial himself was there, collected from the station by Brother Ambrose.

I was surprised when Ambrose walked by me, quiet and serious in himself, scarcely glancing in my direction. I stood to greet Brother Celestine but he motioned me to sit again. Then he sat down beside me. The sun gleamed off the perfect sheen of his trousers. He settled himself, body and mind, into a state of recollection, fingering the creases of his trousers where one knee crossed over the other.

"Matthew," he began and the name troubled me. "I'm glad to find you out here. I have some pretty bad news for you, I'm afraid."

My first thought was they had decided to send me from the Brothers, that I would be even more disgraced at home, that they knew I was unworthy to be one of them. There was that in his voice, a blend of anxiety, sadness and determination that made me feel this was going to be one of the hub points of my whirling, circling life.

"Yes, Brother?"

"It's your family, Matthew, there's been an accident."

He paused, and I looked up at him. In that moment a world of possibilities came and went through my imagination. He hurried on.

"Your mother, Matthew, and your sister, Delia, wasn't that her name ... ?"

That word *"wasn't"* came at me like someone grabbing me violently by the throat, cutting off my breathing.

He glanced at me.

"It seems your father and brother were out with the scythe, taking down the meadows. Your mother and sister were in a loft, shifting last year's hay to clear some space."

He paused. At a loss.

"Yes, that used to be my job," I said, and I rushed at the words. "With a hay-fork, to clear it all to the end of the loft farthest from the door at the end where we'd fork up the new hay from the cart."

"Yes. It seems they had a stove lit in a shed beneath, and a dog or a hen or something must have knocked that over and the hay and straw downstairs caught fire."

Again he paused. I could envision with perfect clarity

the scene, the little shore in the shed where we kept the donkey, the high shelves where the hens roosted, the dark, warm nest of the place which the Tans had violated, the steep wooden staircase to the trapdoor that led into the loft above. Fragrances. Dust-motes. The busy, serious sounds of hens. The restful stirring of the donkey. And how, in the loft, we would shut the trapdoor down in case someone stepped carelessly into the void.

"It seems the ladder to the loft was burned through before the flames penetrated the loft itself. The hay, the wooden floor, rafters ... all went up quickly and furiously."

It was as if an icy wind had begun to blow suddenly from the Atlantic, up from the shore, over the fields and into the sheltered garden. The Brother put his two hands on mine and held me firmly.

"God is good, Matthew, even when we cannot see beyond what our own poor vision allows. Perhaps that is when His love is strongest, when He takes from us, most unexpectedly, those whom we love the most."

"Mother? and Delia?" I whispered.

"Your mother must have been overcome by the smoke, Matthew. She tried to open the trapdoor and of course the smoke would have flooded in. Delia, she was trying to open the end door of the loft but it appears to have had a shutter outside, too?"

"Yes, it used to bang in the wind, in the winter, that awful, persistent sound ... "

"They would have known no pain, Matthew, of that you can be certain. They would have passed out from breathing in that smoke, long before the flames could get to them. When your father and brother got there it was over. The floor of the loft collapsed, your mother, Delia ... I'm sorry, Matthew, I'm deeply sorry. May they rest in peace, good people, both, now in the embrace of Our Lord."

I remember so little of the numbed, slow journey home, Brother Celestine accompanying me down through an Ireland fresh and lush in the fullness of summer. The awful aspect of my home which I had left, it seemed several life-times ago, the blackened, ugly stumps and outcrops of what had been the sheds and loft, the ghostly flitting about of friends and neighbours, the devastation in my father and in Thomas, how we could find no words to offer one another, how the smoking of pipes and the passing round of whiskey and stout among so many crowding out our silences, offered some relief, some postponement of our grieving. I remember how fitting the wailing of the keeners was over the double grave; I had to say some of the prayers above that open hole, trying to maintain some of the dignity of the faith proclaimed by the clothes I wore, how I wanted, instead, to leap down into that neatly sliced grave and scream my guilt, how I should have been with them, to have a shoulder strong enough to burst open the door of the loft into the fresh safe air of my own place, if only … Until the fullness of the earth about me took on an aspect of obscenity, as of some creeping animal gorged on unclean things, waiting to burst open and spew its filth onto our lives.

Gradually those days slowed back into silence. Father continued about his tasks with unnerving fortitude so that I felt more than ever secluded from his person. Thomas, too, was a stranger to me, helping Father, but from his own distance, urging me away whenever I wanted to lend a hand. I know there was no malice in them, no hint of accusation. I had become somebody else, part of something bigger than their lives, something to be revered, from a distance, to be kept apart in the sanctuary that was religion, respected, never envied. They would not let me help, so leaving me to cope with my sorrows in my own, lonely way, as they, men of Ireland, proud, individual, remote, were coping with theirs.

Three or four evenings after that awful burial, when we were sitting in the kitchen after supper, there was a gentle tap at our door. Thomas went to answer it and he recoiled when he saw Manus Cafferky outside. The Cafferkys had not been to the house, the chapel or the graveyard during our tragedy and it was only now, on seeing Manus standing at the door, that I grew aware of that old and bitter world I had left behind.

Father scraped his chair back roughly and stood up, face red with anger, fists bunched.

"Get away from this house in our hour of grief, Manus Cafferky. For you are surely come to gloat!"

"Don't, Father, don't!" I protested, moving swiftly between him and the door.

Manus had grown big and burly; he was red-faced, muscular, but he stood at the door, turning and turning the cap in his hands, looking down at the ground.

"Not at all, sir, not at all," he muttered in response to my father's words. "Me and me father want to offer our honest true sympathy to you and your two sons in your great sorrow. God be good," and he looked up, straight into my father's eyes, "to Mrs Blake and to Delia, Lord have mercy on their souls, they were fine, honest people and very dear to our hearts in the house up above."

The clear sincerity in his voice and demeanour disarmed us. Father stood in the middle of the kitchen, his body proud and erect, but I could feel the urge within him to yield to a paroxysm of grief. His unclenched fists brushed roughly against the texture of his trousers. He nodded, his lips clamped shut, then he turned his back to the door and sat at the table in his place.

Thomas backed out towards the yard as if he had chores to carry out. I looked at this fine young man and all that had been between us, of enmity and hatred, dropped from me. I stretched out my hand in greeting. He looked at me, hesitated, then gripped my hand, and a smile of relief lit up a face I realised was a handsome one. I glanced into the kitchen then went out, drawing the door closed after me.

"I'll walk you down the lane a bit, Manus," I suggested, feeling shyness before him and before the past.

"Thanks, Matt, or should I call you Brother?"

"No, no, not you, my name is Gonzalez now, would you credit that?"

"Gonzalez? By God, that's a name and a half."

We walked slowly side by side down the path; it was dusk; the swifts were still wheeling and scything through the air high above our heads, the needle-points of their cries loud through the linen of the sky. There was an embarrassed silence between us. He was bigger than me now, stronger, and I remembered the fight we had so long ago.

"I'm sorry for all the anger and hurt … " I began.

But he had begun, too, at the same moment: "Matt, I'm truly sorry for your trouble … "

We stopped and turned towards one another. I was astonished to see the powerful bones of his face quivering in grief. He turned quickly away.

"Me and Delia," he spoke it quietly, "we were beginning to be great … "

He let the rest of it float into the evening air.

Then he turned back quickly and blurted out the words:

"Nobody knew a thing about it, mind, nobody ever knew. It was all secret between us. We used to meet above in the woods and sometimes over in the town of Tralee. We were beginning to be great, that's all. We never even kissed, man, we never even touched one another, but by God there was something wonderful about your Delia. It might have been the makings of us all, but for this tragedy. Do you mind, Matt, I mean, about me throwing an eye on Delia? and she on me?"

I took his hand and shook it warmly.

"Manus, I'm heartily delighted to hear it, and I'm the more hurt that all this happened. It must be breaking your heart like it's killing my poor father within. And you're not able to speak to anyone about it."

"And this awful hatred that grew between us, sure they're old, your father and mine, and set in their ways, even though the years move on and the world changes. They won't change. They can't, I suppose. There must be some shift and give in everybody's position, that's what I say."

We walked on a little further. The darkness was falling quickly now. Soon the swifts would disappear into their own quietness and the bats would take over, stitching and unstitching the vest of darkness.

"And you, Manus, how does it stand with you now?"

"Oh, I'm all right, Matt, I'll just take over here until my dad is gone. But my heart isn't in the place, nor in the work here. It's dead, Matt, all of it. I'll probably make it to Dublin or something, you know, help in the fight ... "

"What is your fight, now, Manus?"

He looked at me through the gloom.

"Shifting, Matt, shifting, but in many ways still the same. I'm part of your own Sinn Féin these days."

"I'm surprised to hear that."

"Oh yes, but your Mr de Valera has betrayed us all, though you fought hard for him one fine day."

He laughed, a merry, throaty laugh.

"Sinn Féin are different, now, you know," he went on. We had reached the gate onto the road and stood, shoulder to shoulder, under the archway of escallonia bushes.

"They are the only ones still intent on making Ireland one, and free. A republic, Matt, that's what we wanted, and fought for. O'Higgins was shot last month. I'm not saying there was right or wrong, all I'm saying is that Cosgrave's government were not republican, and that now the only ones left with the ideals are Sinn Féin."

He paused, and began slowly ripping into shreds one of the glossy leaves of the escallonia bush.

"Do you remember, Matt?" he began, looking at me eagerly, "do you remember the Master? Master Brosnan, and what he said? Away back? *Great days, boys, great, holy days. You are going to take your place among the nations of the earth* ... Do you remember?"

"But de Valera," I prodded, "OK he's founded his own party, but he has refused to take the oath."

Manus reached out quickly from the darkness and caught my arm. I could feel the strength of the man in that fierce grip.

"You're wrong, Matt, wrong. De Valera and his gang entered the Dáil the other day, on the eleventh, and they all signed their names in the book."

"Oh no, Manus, oh God, no!"

"They did, de Valera first of all. They took the oath that was the object of their struggles over the years even though, at the same time, they kept saying that in their hearts they were not taking any oath. You can't do that, Matt, you can't do one thing and say it means the opposite."

"No, Manus, no, you can't." I was stunned.

"He's only after power, your lovely de Valera, and he can twist and turn himself into any shape he wants. Next week there's to be a vote of no confidence in Cosgrave. You mark my words. In the next few years de Valera will run this country, Sinn Féin will be walked upon and the hopes for a republic will lie only in the gun and in the back streets."

The monastery in Glenbeg, that place of refuge, surfaced before my mind and a yearning to return flooded over me. Again I took Manus's hand and shook it, eager to erase the past, to acknowledge his honesty and integrity, eager to share his revulsion over the slithering and posturing of politicians. Out of the warmth of that night came the association in my mind of Delia's and my mother's death with the untruth of de Valera and of the changeling Fianna Fáil.

"We're on the same side again, then, Manus," I said.

He laughed, with quiet satisfaction.

"I'm glad, Matt, I'm very glad. And maybe we should never breathe a word of what might have been between poor Delia and myself – they mightn't ever be able to understand it around here."

"I won't betray your trust, you can be certain of that."

"Goodnight, so, Matt", he whispered and I warmed at the old familiar glow of affection between us. He closed the clasp of the gate. Then I heard him chuckle as he headed away into the night:

"Gonzalez! Gonzalez! Well did you ever, Gonzalez! did you ever … ?"

DAVID

ONE AFTERNOON, I WAS SITTING HIGH IN ONE OF THE TREES OF THE grove beside the house, spying on the poor earthlings going about their tasks below. I saw Jack McHugh and his son Padraig, coming up the hill towards our house from the village. They stopped outside our gate and I could see the agitation in Jack's movements, he was shifting from one foot to the other as if the ground he walked on was on fire. Every so often he watched out down the road. I heard Father's car coming and when it turned in at the gate Jack jumped forward and opened the door of the car, so eager was he to meet my father.

They spoke together for a while and I couldn't hear the words. I began to clamber down from the tree.

As I came out from the shadows Father was hurrying from the house, his rifle in his hand. He grinned at me.

"Want to see a bit of shooting?"

He strode ahead of me onto the road, turned left and up the hill towards the bogs. Soon he stepped off the road, over a cart track that crossed rough commonage near Loughnaneaneen. I saw two men waiting out in the bog, a horse standing beside them. Father was silent, striding out with Jack and Padraig, I trailing behind. When we got near I could see that the horse's front leg was broken and hanging useless. At the other side of the horse they had dug a deep hole, the wet peat piled up on the far side. I looked down into it, there was a pool of water, the bottom was black and soggy, and there were neat nicks down along the side of the bog where the sleán had been expertly used. Around us everything was waste land, bog, heathers, hillocks, an occasional bog-deal root standing like a dinosaur. In the near distance rose the slopes of Mweelin mountain and above us the vast sky over Achill. There were clouds, grey and heavy, ominous.

Father moved away from the horse, and called me to come stand by him. He put a cartridge in the gun. I could see the horse, standing alongside the hole, his eye wide but calm, as if he knew his strange hour had come round at last, and that this was to be his place, this his time. Jack stood awhile near his head, patting him, whispering to him, while the two men backed away; then Jack moved back, glanced towards my father and nodded his head, slowly. The horse stood alone, patient, the tail gently flicking.

Father raised the rifle; I put my fingers in my ears, waiting for the awful crack of the shot. Nothing happened. Father was standing there, perfectly still, the rifle raised, the barrel steady. I knew where his aim would be, that small patch behind the horse's eye, but there was only a long silence, then he lowered the rifle again. I felt ashamed of him, why didn't he do it? There was expectation all around, from horse and men, from the very hills in their waiting.

I lowered my hands and half-turned from him. Was he scared? I looked away towards the trees of the grove and I wanted to be back there, up in that hide-away I had high in the tree, alone and silent amongst pine needles and shifting breezes, living like a branch, a leaf, scenting the resin …

And then came the awful rattle of the shot. I turned quickly. The afternoon seemed to burst apart with the noise, I could hear the sound of the shot expand and reverberate through the low hills, as if it could have shaken them to their very roots. I looked towards the horse.

It had not stirred. I could see, from the corner of my eye, that Father had already lowered his rifle. There was a faint misting of smoke from the barrel. He had missed! and again came that shame over me, followed by a desire to laugh, to shrug, to think well, what does it matter anyway? But, slowly, slowly, that great eye still open, the horse began to keel over, as a wall keels over, stiffly, upright and dignified, until it disappeared into that awful hole.

It was the sound the heavy, fleshy body made when it slapped the water in the bottom of the hole that disturbed me most. The dreadful wet thud of it seemed to run right through the earth under my feet; the sound echoed again, like the shot had, through the afternoon. I shuddered with a fear that has not left me since, a fear of death, a sorrow, too, that the great cart-horse must rot in the wet, cold embrace of that sucking peat. That sound, that echoing slap, continues to echo in my brain, a source of nightmare.

Father had gone up to the hole with the other men and stood, looking down. I could not go and look. He ejected the spent cartridge and turned back towards me, smiling. I think he muttered the word "Perfect!" to somebody, or to himself. Then he strode past me, without speaking, and I followed him towards home.

MATTHEW

I SPOKE TO MOTHER AND DELIA WITH A CERTAINTY OF THEIR presence. I knew that the reconciliation with Manus was of Delia's making, that the calmness and certainty I felt were thanks to the presence of my mother. I believed that only suffering can excise the human imperfections to which the flesh is subject. And the mind. I saw the fire as their Purgatory. They had gone, then, perfected, into the presence of that God to whose service I returned with determination.

On the train back to Derry, I dozed, the rattling settled to a pleasant rhythm, trees and bushes on either side of the carriages merging into a green blur, smoke and smuts from the engine blew all around. The windows were closed. I slept. Delia was in the carriage with me, laughing and scolding, and all at once she began to hoist her skirts up slowly, grinning at me, mocking, above her knees, up along her thighs, and she was dancing, the white of her flesh showing, she was swaying libidinously, smiling with pleasure, with an exultation that kept me mesmerised. Manus too, was in the carriage, sneering, and this dance was for his gratification. I could see Mother coming across the fields towards the train, floating over fences and bushes, angry. Manus grabbed my arm and pushed a rifle into my hands:

"You're the expert," he whispered to me, pointing at my mother. He lowered the strap on the window and I laid the barrel on it and aimed; Mother kept waving frantically at us. I touched the trigger, that loving touch, and tried to sense where her pain was.

I woke, screaming; an elderly gentleman sitting opposite was reaching both arms towards me as if I was about to fall off the seat. I was frantic for a moment, I was hot, the black suit, pullover, stock, the collar, the imprisonment ...

"There is a terrible thing bursting inside me," I said to Ambrose. "To do with Delia and with Mother."

"Suffering and loss, Matthew," he began at once (we were walking, a blackberry-rich, late warm September afternoon, on a long sandy lane that ended by the harbour) "are the echoes of living; they will die away, but very, very slowly."

"I think this particular grief will last forever."

"What kind of a son, what kind of a brother would you be if, after just a few weeks, you didn't know such grief?"

"But this is more, much more; this is guilt, too."

"Guilt? For what, Matthew?"

"If I hadn't joined the Brothers I'd have been there in the loft, there would have been no fire, Mother and Delia would still be alive. I pray every day, Ambrose, for the repose of their souls. Yet what I think I really am praying for is forgiveness, maybe the guilt I feel is that I'm not sufficiently good as a Christian Brother to balance their death in some way. To stop the fact of their suffering. Anyway, what's the point of praying for something that's long over, you can't alter the facts, you cannot touch history, no matter how hard you pray."

We came out from behind a fuchsia hedge and there was a sudden view of the pier, and out on the sea the islands were visible. We stopped, stricken again with the immensity about us. I could feel, too, that Ambrose was girding himself for an answer. He climbed, clumsily, but chuckling at himself, over a low ditch, I followed, and we sat on rocks, facing the sea. He picked a blade of grass heavy with seed, he scattered the seed into the breeze, then shifted himself determinedly.

"Prayer, Gonzalez, is our direct channel to God. It has to do with us trying to reach out of our pathetic smallness into the mystery of God. It's to do with nothingness and allness, with time and eternity, with a part and with the whole. There's no good trying to make yourself believe that what has happened maybe didn't happen. It has happened! An event. An event in time, time has moved on from that point, and that's that."

He was looking down at the grass between his feet. He was screwing his face, his whole body, into this effort, and I stayed still, close to his breathing. Trusting him.

"Time," he repeated. "That's us. Humans. Who can only understand things in terms of time, linear, one thing happening after another. But you must remember that God is not bound by time. He created the universe and He is not limited by the work of His own hands. God is outside time. Outside the linear. For Him there's no before and after an event. Where He is, that's eternity. Are you with me?"

"Yes," I breathed, quietly.

"Right. Now. You cannot ask God to undo an event that has happened in time. Because that would be a travesty of His creating idea. But you surely can pray to Him to have the qualities of that event such that they may not actually have been so bad. Do you follow me?"

"No, Ambrose."

I could see the frustration stirring his body as he gathered his mind towards the task.

"God is outside the limited circle that time necessarily is. So that, being outside of it, He can change, or manipulate, or influence the past, the present and the future because for Him it's all there, like the island in the ocean before His vision. Now if time is like a fence stitching all of our events together, He can reach out and touch the fence at any point, past, present or future, even though we only see a tiny section of that fence, a bit of the past, a bit of the present, and we cannot really see even a tiny bit into the future. So if you call to Him from a point along the fence, and ask Him to see to it that the qualities of a point in the fence we have passed by may be such and such, then that is perfectly possible, logical and reasonable, even to our puny minds."

He stopped. He was breathing as if he had climbed a steep hill. But he was elated, too, and I was beginning to feel some understanding.

"So, Matthew, let's look at Delia and Mrs Blake. Right, several weeks ago, died in a fire. Time. Gone. Cannot be changed as a fact. But we cannot know the qualities of that event in their fullness. If you pray to God now, at this point, that Delia and your mother may not have suffered, then, there's every reason to believe that God will answer your prayer out of time in His eternal position. Not altering the facts, not taking a post out of the fence, but anticipating your prayer and influencing the qualities of that event. In His goodness seeing the prayers already in OUR future, taking them into account in OUR past, and affecting the qualities of the suffering of His children out of His eternity. Do you follow me, Matt?"

"Yes, Ambrose. We're chasing in a circle, God can reach in at any moment and touch the qualities of the points in the circle. Past, present and future are all *now* to Him. So I can keep praying to Him to lessen the sufferings of Delia and Mother and what I pray for now and next week He will have already taken into account … or something … "

I felt as if I had got some grip on things from this simple, plump man whom I cherished and believed in as a

brother. I wanted to embrace him, to convey my sense of
loving him in some way, but how could I do that? I said:

"I'm grateful, Ambrose. Thank you. Thank you, for
Delia, for my mother. I will pray for them, and I will
always pray to them, too, because they are present. The
dead must be with us the way God is with us. Always."

The sharp, elusive snipe of hurt had been sighted. I
knew the grief would be there but I felt, at that moment,
more in control than I had been before.

It was several weeks later that I was sitting in the chapel of
Our Lady, Queen of the Sea, praying, musing, dozing. The
low sunlight of evening coloured me and the benches
through the stained window.

I came alert suddenly; I murmured, aloud, Mother's and
Delia's names in a quick invocation. Then I heard the
sound again: the sound of a gunshot. In spite of my long
period of inertia and dullness, the sound sent a thrill of
excitement through me. Then there was silence.

I came out the Church door onto the moor that led over
rocks and scrubland to the cliffs and the sea. The air was
still and warm; a wheatear, bobbing its bird body on a rock
nearby, scolded me and the world, then flew off into the
heathers. I stood, my black hat held at my side, waiting. I
heard another shot and felt I could locate the direction the
sound came from. In those times the IRA seemed to be the
only people working for a republic, in spite of de Valera's
woolly pronouncements of the aims of Fianna Fáil. There
was talk, that year, of the government bringing in a Public
Safety Act that would make the IRA illegal; there was talk
of the death penalty; there had been shootings, the
undertow of unrest was palpable. There would be shooting
practice.

I went cautiously up the hill towards a wood of furze
bushes. I suspected illegal drilling activity of which I had

heard and as I approached, the old feeling of excitement came back to me as when I carried the gun across the hill to my father. There was a small wood of alders beyond the furze and as I approached I could hear voices. There was a fourth shot and a scream that was quickly stifled. This was no practice, no drilling, no innocent hunting party.

I kept the thickest of the trees between me and the voices. Slowly I got nearer. The voices were low and hurried. There was a shout of terror :

"No! No! Please!"

and then another shot. The echo of that shot seemed to linger a long time, like a spirit, hovering over the trees. Then two men came hurriedly in my direction. I drew back into the shelter of the trees. Two figures passed me, within feet of where I stood. One was small, stout and baldheaded. He held a revolver in one hand. The other was Ambrose Mulcahy, Christian Brother. They paused before emerging from the shelter of the alders, looking across the deserted moor, towards and beyond the Chapel. Then they moved away, the bald-headed man putting the gun inside his jacket. I was mouthing Delia's name and Mother's, as a prayer, as a plea.

I stood still until both men disappeared beyond the chapel. They did not look back. I went in through the trees. It took me a while to find what I knew I'd find. The undergrowth was dense but there was a small pathway trodden through it. About fifty yards through the trees there was a small clearing where the growth was trampled hard. There was a man tied to the bole of a tree, his hands tied together above his head, a rope around his waist, another tying his legs to the tree. I thought of Robbie Hake and instantly the pounding in my chest began. I could see he had been shot in both knees. The trousers were torn at the knees and there was blood, dark red, staining the cloth. His head was hanging to one side, the side of his skull a mess of blood and gore. I was sick at once, doubling up on the ground before the horror of it. I retched several times, not daring to look again at the poor tortured body on the tree.

I got back somehow to the monastery, meeting nobody on the way. I opened the front door and went down the hallway past the parlour and the office. I made my way up the stairs, holding the banisters, dragging myself along. I got into the bathroom at the end of the landing and undressed, plunging my face and hands into a basin of cold water, scrubbing my body from head to foot. I sat a while on the toilet seat, shivering; then I towelled myself until warmth rose through me. I put on my drawers and vest, took the rest of my clothes in my arms, unlocked the bathroom and got to my room without being seen. I fell on the bed, unclear as to what I ought to do.

I lay, smoking, memories and images racing through my mind. The pain high in my chest was a dull and regular pounding at the background of my thoughts. The evening darkened and I lay on. Soon the room was dark, only the glow of the tip of my cigarette when I drew on it, or the sudden flaring of a match. I could put no order on my thinking.

When a gentle knock came on the door I jumped with the fright of it. I shouted, "Leave me alone!" There was silence. I thought the person had gone and I began to light another cigarette. I was unable to find the box of matches so I reached to put on the light. Brother Ambrose was standing at the foot of the bed!

He grinned into my face. I was cold, startled, afraid. I saw the matches on the floor and reached for them. I lit a cigarette and offered him the pack. He shook his head. Then he raised his hand.

"Your hat," he said, "I found it outside the Queen of the Sea. You were praying. You heard shots. I saw you heading back. I followed you, Matthew, to see what you were going to do, where you'd go."

I stared at him, feeling that this was all unreal.

"Funny, Ambrose," I said, "I don't know your name?"

He chuckled and left my hat on the chair. Then he picked up my clothes from the floor, piece by piece, and left them neatly over the back of the chair. He put my shoes, side by side, in under the chair, muttering, "Dirty, dirty, need a good cleaning, all this lot."

Then he picked my overcoat from the back of the door and threw it on the bed.

"Put it on, Matthew, no use getting pneumonia at this stage of your career."

"What's your name, Ambrose, your real name?"

He sat down heavily on the side of the bed.

"You know, I've almost forgotten it, I've been simple Ambrose for so long. It's not a great name, Edward, or Ned, if you like, and at home I was often known as Eamon. I preferred that. I was teased a lot, too, because I was round and plump and they called me Pudding. Funny thing, a name, makes you act in a certain way, don't you think? I still think of myself as Eamon. Irish. Proud of it, you know, until that big tall American made it a curse to this country. But the name remains deep inside me, Matthew, this old sad country of ours. It's deep inside. And I can't still its calling."

He paused. I drew the coat up over my body. I was not afraid of him now, how could I be?

"I'd like to understand, Ambrose? What about integrity, doesn't that count for anything? Who was that man you killed? And why?"

He drew himself upright, sighing deeply. Then he reached over and switched off the light. The darkness yielded slowly and faintly to an autumn moon. I could scarcely see the outlines of the black-suited man beside me.

"One thing, Matthew, straight off, I do not use a gun. Ever."

"Who was that other man?"

"You don't need to know him. He's well up in the Irish Republican Army in these parts. He's a patriot, Matthew, like me, like you, too, I suspect, he's unhappy about the carving up of our country."

Ambrose paused again.

"He's a murderer, Ambrose, and you tortured that man up there."

"Murder, no, no, not murder, and for the sake of the lives of many others we had to get information from that man. There was a raid on the barracks in Sligo last week, you remember? an attempt to get weapons. When the men arrived it was clear they were expected! Three arrests, Matthew, Irish men throwing Irish men in gaol! There was a traitor, and now there is one traitor less amongst us."

"But one of the policemen in the barracks in Sligo was killed, Ambrose, and he was an Irish man too!"

"That's the sad, sad part of it, Matthew. Those that take the florins instead of freedom have to suffer the consequences. Remember what they wrote, Pearse, and Plunkett, and the others, remember? *We place the cause of the Irish republic under the protection of the Most High God, whose blessing we invoke upon our arms, and we pray that no one who serves that cause will dishonour it by cowardice, inhumanity, or rapine.* It's beautiful, Matthew, isn't it? *In this supreme hour the Irish nation must, by its valour and discipline, and by the readiness of its children to sacrifice themselves for the common good, prove itself worthy of the august destiny to which it is called.* Sacrifice, Matthew, there's the word, we must be willing to sacrifice ourselves and others for this noble cause."

There was silence between us for a while. Ambrose had spoken sadly, I knew that somewhere inside me something agreed with him.

"There were five shots, Ambrose, I heard five shots. At least."

"He was a fool, that man, but he was brave. On the wrong side, blind, but courageous. Two shots at first, one over his head, one into the ground at his feet. He would tell us nothing. Then one into his right knee, Matthew. That was all I wanted done. If he would not speak then, I knew he would never speak. He said nothing. And I have no power, Matthew, none at all. Anyway, as the commander said, he had seen us, and he knew me. I'm sorry he had to die."

"I would never have believed, Ambrose, that you, you … "

"You don't put off your Irishness when you put away your layman's clothes. And it's a holy, righteous cause, Matthew, if we don't get it right now it will cause anguish for generations to come. Cosgrave doesn't dare, Matthew, and de Valera prevaricates. They only want power, those in politics. It's up to the people to fight for freedom. I am of the people, Matthew, and I always will be."

We were silent again for a time.

"I suppose, deep down, I agree with some of what you say, Ambrose. But death, there have been so many deaths! and they achieve nothing, nothing but pain and distress and bitterness."

"Ah, Matthew, Matthew, Matthew, you are obsessed with the dead. There will always be ghosts about your life, poor man. We spoke, remember? about the dead. You pray for them, Matthew, you pray for the dead and you ask God that they may not have suffered. And I will pray for that foolish, courageous man up on the hill. But that is all, Matthew, that is all. The dead are dead. You must let them go, let them go. Think of them as small, perfect boats, waiting at the shore; they have hoisted sail and are waiting, waiting until we, the living, earthbound creatures, are strong enough to cut the last ropes that hold them back. Let them go, they will drift away, silently, drifting away in the moonlight over a perfect sea. They have to begin their own voyage; they are imperfect still, selfish, stubborn, attached to the putrefying objects they have known. We are all attached to putrefaction, Matthew, and it is only death that will begin our release. Death? a gift, Matthew, a gift! Let them go, let your mother and sister go, let this poor broken soul go, too, free them and you will free yourself. Take a step out towards the great and exhilarating darkness of eternity!"

I imagined his face, in the blackness of the room, animated and alert, his eyes big with excitement, that small, stumpy body without grace.

"So, Matthew," he breathed at me after a while. "What are you going to do?"

"About what, Eamon?"

"Hah! Eamon is it? sounds great in your mouth, Matthew, fills me with sadness and nostalgia, God forgive me! Answer me now. What are you going to do?"

There was quietness in his voice, no sense of threat or anger, not even of sadness.

"Nothing, I suppose, because I know I feel the way you do about our country. But I cannot agree with murder, that can only lead to more killing. But I see no good coming from my telling of this crime to anyone."

"Good, Matthew, good, and wise. Maybe some day soon, when you free yourself from the nets you have wrapped yourself in, maybe you'll do something to help?"

He reached to me, out of the darkness, and touched me on the forehead. It was a gesture of affection and yet, suddenly, I feared him and resented the contact. He sighed again, got up and murmured, "Goodnight, Brother Gonzalez", then he was gone, light from the landing outside slicing for a moment through the opened door, then vanishing again. I stayed on the bed, the black overcoat of the Brothers covering me. I stared out on darkness, my thoughts shifting like smoke blown from a chimney, tattered and flung into a wild, unfriendly sky.

DAVID

As in a book of origins, he comes
striding down a long, cleft valley,
cartridge-belts ebullient across his chest,
the rifle riding gently on his arm;
mountains lift their names about him –
Bunowna, Croghaun, Bunnafreva, Keem;

clouds rip themselves against high craglands;
I, cowering somewhere in his potency,
hear the distant pounding of the ocean,
the sky is filled with all the space
between Achill and America;
up in the hills, the mountain goats run free;

the soft peat floor is treacherous,
eager, like time, to take its prey
and hold it in its juices; he has climbed
cliff-slopes salted with gull-droppings,
and paused by the thosts of old stone boleys;
I whisper my name into the bowl of time –

his head jerks upwards, and he frowns.

The long hay-loft was low
and raftered like the island chapel;
among the undersides of slates,
snow-falls of ageing plaster, star-holes,

he taught me how to climb from beam to beam,
my feet never touching the ground;

he showed me how to fall, cat-soft
into mothering hay, and I never dreamed
the rough stone floor of the future;
once I dressed up to look like him,
strutting with waders, cartridge-belts and rifle;
now he is in my words, my diffidence,

he has been dressing himself again in my flesh.

It is easy to say "I love you" to the dead,
the words are a hard, packed ball
beaten and beaten against a high, blank wall;
but he whispers his name to me still, comes
striding down a long, cleft, valley,
mountains lifting their names about him –

Bunowna, Croghaun, Bunnafreva, Keem.

FIVE

MATTHEW

THE FIRST, PREMONITORY RAINS OF WINTER HAD ALREADY STRUCK.
The only warmth I could find was in the monastery chapel
in the mornings. It was dark when we came down for
morning prayers and Mass. I wore my coat over my
soutane. There was shuffling, and gentle preparations
about the altar, the scraping of a match to light the big
candles, the removal and folding away of the green altar
cloth.

Introibo ad altare Dei.

Ad Deum qui laetificat juventutem meum.

As I tried to loosen my grip on Mother and on Delia I
knew that the years of my youth had vanished, swiftly and
silently. The word "joy" was unfamiliar to me now. I was
clothed in black, in darkness, the light of candles and of
the sanctuary lamp could dispel none of that darkness.

Ambrose knelt, answering the Latin prayers.

Agnus Dei qui tollis peccata mundi,

Dona nobis pacem.

He rose, at the due moment, stepped out from his prie-
dieu, genuflected, approached the altar rails with

exemplary devotion. When the acolyte held the golden paten under Ambrose's chin, when the brother closed his eyes and raised his head devoutly, his tongue offered to receive his God, my heart quailed inside me.

I sat in the sanctuary of the little chapel of Our Lady Queen of the Sea. I was crying, somewhere far within myself. There was no sound anywhere. Only the occasional creak of a bench or the sigh of a stone settling further into its place within the walls. The great wheel of time lumbered on. Light was dulled through the stained windows. My instinct was to scream out the names of Mother and of Delia and to couple the scream with a blasphemy against my vanished God. It is not easy to release the dead into their destiny when all your being is concentrated on the isolation of your own weight and presence. Watching your own, screaming face turned towards you.

I walked back to the monastery. I packed my old brown suitcase with what was mine. It was evening, but I left at once, meeting nobody, walking out that small front garden path, closing the wicket gate, passing the neatly ordered graves of the Brothers, up the long avenue to the road. I spent the night in the luxury of a room in the Royal Hotel, slept warm and deep and was in Dublin next evening. I indulged myself in one night in the Gresham Hotel. The porters looked at me with unfeigned curiosity, looked at my sad bag, and I was asked to pay in advance. I did so. At once a young porter doffed his hat, snatched my bag and I followed him, like a lord, up the broad sweep of the marble staircase.

I owned a spinning top once, as a child. It was a tin affair, brightly painted with birds, monkeys, giraffes, clowns; about the figures of living creatures that skirted the broad belly of the top there were lovely geometric shapes, diamonds and circles, squares and triangles.

Underneath the band was a long line of swimming ducks, beak to tail, tail to beak. The handle of the top was made of wood, smooth, rounded, perfect to the touch, painted red. The base on which it had to spin was of a glittering metal, like the tip of an arrow. You pressed the handle on its metal spiral, pressed and pressed, pumped faster and faster, until, when you let it go, the whole thing spun, all the painted shapes and colours merging into daffodil yellow, while a high, musical note came from it. It clattered to a halt, falling ignominiously to one side and veering drunkenly about the floor. Then it lay, ugly, pointless, a meaningless amalgam of craftsmanship, effort and thought.

I bought clothes in Clery's. To change clothes is easy. To change direction easy, too. But to find a new place to live in where your own presence causes you no pain, that is not so easy. You do not put off your troubles with your clothes. I was no longer a Christian Brother. I was nothing. They had let me go, reluctantly, and for that much I was grateful; but what was I now? Oh yes, they had made a teacher out of me, they would offer me help in starting out again ... but I was lost.

I wandered the streets of the city. Everywhere the reek of poverty greeted me, children in torn clothes, unwashed, held their hands out for charity. Men and women hurried everywhere as if they were being pursued, or were in pursuit. Only along the gas-lit central streets was there any leisure apparent, any sense of joy, or hope. Several times I stood on the bridge over the Liffey, perhaps to watch a Guinness barge work its way towards the port and the sense of that dark, full water offering release rose in me. I was terrified, then, terrified of myself and the lethargy that had settled on me. I could not go home to Drumdouglas. That was impossible.

I hesitated under the high blank walls of St Martin's

Hospital. Then, with difficulty, I walked through the great iron gates, up the cobblestone avenue to the door. There was a man dressed in a porter's uniform sitting behind a hatch.

"Excuse me. I wonder if I could see Sylvia Doran, please?"

"A patient? Visiting hours are two to three and seven to eight."

"No, no. She's a nurse."

"Is she on duty?"

"I don't know, I'm afraid, I just, em, called … "

He gazed at me suspiciously. I looked away, sniffling and rubbing at my nose with my hand.

"I'll call the station," he said and got up to leave his little cell. Then he asked:

"By the way, what name will I give?"

"Thanks. Tell her, Matthew Blake. Though I don't know if she'll remember. No. Better if you don't leave a name. Just, if you could find out if she's on duty and what time she's finished."

For a moment I thought I had been too bold. He stopped and looked at me, putting his two hands into the pockets of his overalls. He considered a moment, then turned and moved slowly down a corridor. I stepped out of the hallway, back into the open air under the great, forbidding façade of the building. Daws and starlings were squabbling everywhere. Above the tops of old chestnut trees I could see an army of dark clouds crossing the sky. For a moment I panicked; I could vanish now and forget all of this. But I held firm, the knowledge of that vast, impersonal blank city beyond those walls terrifying me.

He came back into the hallway and tossed the words towards me, indifferently, like ash.

"She's not finished till eight o'clock tonight."

Then he opened the door into his office and that was that.

At a quarter to eight I stood in near-darkness under the arch of the gateway. It was cold and I was dressed lightly. I took short dashing walks up and down the street, watched everyone who came in or left the hospital. The cigarette butts began to gather about my feet.

Then, suddenly, she was there, leaving the hospital with a few companions. I stepped back into the darkness and she turned past me, going quickly up the street. I followed, hesitant to call her name among the others. They walked a while, crossed the river and separated. Sylvia, her long grey coat hiding her form, hurried by the low wall along the river. Once she turned, abstractedly, as if she was aware of a presence, but her glance blew past me like a breeze.

She reached O'Connell Bridge and paused, waiting to cross. I came up beside her, then, and spoke her name.

She turned. Once again I was stricken by her beauty, that young, flawless face, eager and bright, the fine, strong features, the eyes big and clear and lovely.

"Yes?"

"You don't remember me? I'm Matthew Blake, I was a patient; you were very kind to me. Do you remember?"

She reached her hand to me at once and touched me on the arm. Her face grew warm as she smiled.

"Matthew. Of course I remember. Matthew Blake. Well, well, well. But I thought you were with the Brothers?"

I was filled with delight that she remembered. I shuffled restlessly beside her. Would she reject me as a failure? She had turned and was watching the carriages, cars and trams coming along the bridge. Then she stepped onto the road and I followed.

"I have to catch the 8.30 train," she said, smiling brightly towards me.

She agreed to meet me for lunch the following day and I watched as she went down the river walk towards the station, turning once to wave. The moon was low over the sea, hanging just over the railway bridge across the Liffey. The city was bathed in a gentle yellow light and the sounds of cars and trams, the murmuring of the evening crowds, was soothing to me, soft and gentle as lake water.

We met, sometimes for lunch, sometimes in the evening when I walked her from the hospital to the station. But I was ignorant and hesitant, treasuring her company, scared of doing or saying anything that might send her scurrying away from my mixed-up life. Until she asked me if I would accompany her home one evening. I was staying with the Brothers until they could arrange something for me in one of their schools; I could not ask her to the monastery!

It was barely eight o'clock when I climbed the steps to the station. The evening was dark and warm, as if the sky had become a blanket, warm and woolly, drawn over the city. The light from the gaslamps was reflected in the water of the river and shimmered gently with the shivering of the gas and the slow movement of the water. I bought a return ticket and walked out onto the platform to wait for her. The view of the tracks moving out northwards into the darkness of a great curving bridge, and southwards, rounding the high walls of the station and vanishing into the tangle of the suburbs and the future, made me restless with excitement. I walked up and down the platform, waiting. Every minute that passed was ages long.

At last I heard the shunting and shushing of the train heading out over the bridge, like a great shout of encouragement and at the same moment Sylvia appeared, flushed and breathless after running up the steps. Her face was lovely in the half-light and she smiled brightly and caught my arm. She hurried me along the platform as the engine appeared at the end of the bridge, its blackness growing into an image of power as steam came sucking from around the great flanged wheels and rhythmic puffs rushed aggressively from its funnel. It clashed and hissed and jangled to a stop.

I gripped the handle of the carriage and whipped open the door. Several people got out, leaving the carriage almost empty. We clambered in, like children setting out on a day's picnic and I slammed the door shut behind us.

The train was a great black monster climbing along the backs of the houses and we looked down into gardens and back yards, and thundered over the road into Westland Row. I glanced several times at the elderly man and woman sitting facing each other at the other side of the carriage; they looked stern, sat perfectly upright and still, each gazing vacantly at a spot on the wall behind the other's head. Sylvia and I watched each other, and smiled.

Half an hour later the train drew in to Sydney Parade. I let the window fall, leaned out and grabbed the door-handle. A guard was shouting something up at the far end of the platform. The high whining voice tuned with boredom was ghostlike in the dim light. I stepped out and helped Sylvia down from the carriage. As I slammed the door shut I saw that the elderly couple had not shifted their positions. I pitied them. Their lives grounded in absences and silence, mine about to burst into light. As I held the door and gazed at them I was aware of the great expanse of the universe waiting when I turned.

We walked out onto a road lined with trees. It was dark and still. It could have been a country road we were on and I reached bravely and took Sylvia by the elbow.

"You'd need somebody to mind you here," I mumbled.

Sylvia laughed and reached her arm about my waist.

"I could find my way blindfolded," she said.

We passed the opening of a laneway. I could make out a row of small houses with one street lamp somewhere in the distance.

"I live down there," she pointed.

I hesitated but she kept walking, past the laneway, on

into the darkness.

"Come on!" she laughed, "I've a surprise for you, down here a little way."

I could hear the faint sounds of the city. I held Sylvia's hand and we walked quickly under the trees, turned a bend and there was the sea stretching away to a silver horizon.

"Sandymount Strand!" she announced. There was a low stone wall and a gap through which she passed. There was a wide strand, lights gathered on a headland away to our right, the lights of the city a sickly yellow to the left and out over the sea, in the distance, the faint lights of Howth. I stood in a basin of wonder, the stillness and warmth of the evening, the beauty of the woman beside me, confused humming of memories in my brain. There was a gentle rumour from the sea.

"It's wonderful," I whispered. She squeezed my hand.

We began to walk across the sand.

"I'm sure there were crowds of people here today," she said, "you can feel the warmth they left behind, and if you listen you can hear echoes of their laughter."

A wall loomed ahead of us.

"The baths," she said, leading me around to one side. "The tide goes very far out from here, so far you'd need a bicycle to reach it and then to race it back in. It returns at a great speed. Like a horse."

There was an iron gate in the wall. Sylvia reached and rattled it. It opened. She laughed.

"Come on!" she said. "They often leave it open at night."

She drew me in and closed the gate quietly after us. We stood as in a high-walled garden, open to the heavens, a pool of sea-water for a meadow.

Sylvia was excited, and giggling.

"Can you swim?" she whispered. She was unbuttoning

the dress at her neck. I was alarmed.

"You're not swimming now, are you?" I stammered.

She laughed at me.

"It'll be warm," she said, "we'll have it all to ourselves."

She was undressing rapidly, the flowered dress had already dropped onto the concrete floor at the side of the pool. She stood there, her arms raised to remove her scarf, the white sheen of her slip making her a ghost before me.

"But I have no swimming-clothes," I protested. There was a gnawing fear in my stomach and all my senses were strained and tense.

"What matter?" she laughed, "there's nobody to see."

"You're not going … naked, are you?"

The word was hard and frightening in my mouth. She had kicked off her shoes and pulled the slip over her thighs to release her stockings.

"Come on!" she urged, "we can slide into the water without a sound. I've come down here on my own often before. To clean away the dust of the city. It's wonderful! you feel free and rich as if you owned the universe."

"But," I stammered, lost, "we can't be naked … "

"Why not?" she said. And then she laughed. "Sure haven't I seen you naked before, and worse than naked, too, God help you."

She was leaning back against the wall now, drawing off her nylon stockings. Suddenly she had caught the hem of her slip and had drawn it up quickly over her head; raising her arms high she took it off and flung it on top of her crumpled dress. She stood in bra and pants, full-bodied, demanding.

I tried to unbutton my jacket. I laid it down beside her clothes, folding it carefully.

"Last one in's a rotten fish!" she whispered and I could see the lovely curves of her calves, the soft resting-places of her hocks, the filling wonder of her thighs; her flesh gleamed in the light reflected from the sky but my whole body was held in an unyielding grip and a blockage caught my throat, making me unable to speak. I stood up again, lifting my jacket in my hands.

She reached her hands behind her back and unclasped her bra. Unhesitatingly she let it drop from her and threw it on top of her clothes. Her breasts were full and firm, the nipples dark.

"Matthew," she said, "come on, quickly. Don't stand there as if you had seen a ghost."

She watched while I put down my jacket again. I straightened and began to loosen my tie. With one quick movement she had her pants off and stood, naked, before me.

"There!" she said quietly, "I'm ready."

"I can't, I can't," I managed to stammer, and I reached down again for my jacket. I began to put it on, trying not to look at her.

"It's wrong, it's wrong, wrong … " I muttered.

She picked up her slip and held it in front of her. I was backing, foolishly, towards the gate.

"It's you who are wrong, Matthew", she said, irritably. "It's you who are wrong. Your life is full of ghosts, can you not face into the world like a man?"

There was anger in her now, and the beginning of contempt. I felt all I had ever known of life crumble rapidly about me. In desperation I clutched, grasping at the years of my past. And the word that came out fell from me, as unthinkingly as a breath, the word "Whore!"

Oh God! I was drowning, too far from the shore I had walked on for so many years, so out of breath in this new world, so incapable. She reached quickly and hit me, hard, across the face. I fell back against the iron gate.

"You damned fool, go! go! get away from me, get out of my life, you are sick, Matthew, sick."

I opened the gate and ran, stumbling across the sand towards the welcoming darkness of the trees, my cheek stinging, hot tears in my eyes, my life a scarlet flame of unhappiness and loss. I stumbled over the low stone wall and out onto the road. I turned quickly towards the city and half-walked, half-ran away from her and from myself, heading towards the Martello tower that loomed like a protective presence ahead of me. Only once did I turn back, but I could see nothing, only the blackness of space empty under the darkness of the night.

DAVID

Old man, in corded, ripe-plum dressing-gown,
sitting out, and silent; beyond high windows
are blood-bright tulips, funerary
wind-blown daffodils. Love comes

blundering about him; he
holds himself apart, intent upon his going,
abandons me mid-season, my words
all, like petals, falling about my feet.

MATTHEW

HOW FAR DO YOU RUN TO FIND A PLACE WHERE YOU CAN ESCAPE from yourself? The Brothers, although I was no longer one of them, offered me a teaching position in Dublin, or one in Donegal. I chose Donegal and escaped as quickly as I could.

Assistant teacher in Carrickmore, no onerous task! I soon found comfort, staying with Eddie and Nora Blackshaw and their grown-up, bachelor son, Charlie, outside the village of Killybegs. Each morning I cycled five miles to Carrickmore, winds and rains, the harsh hills and exhilarating valleys of the country road pushing my body to well-being.

Charlie was a fisherman and vanished for days on end, out to face his own exhilarating hills and hollows in the sea. I was left with the elders, both of them settled into routines of minor drudgery and major devotions. I had stepped out of my own untidy past, out of its terrain, its wheeling, into dullness. To become a tree, wood and branch, to raise lethargic muscles in the spring, to take and absorb whatever rain or sunshine that was offered and respond with perfect passivity. And in the winter to withdraw, to curl into myself and hoard what I had gained until the sun should come again.

I had a back room upstairs in the home of the Blackshaws and it looked out over an acre of scutch-grass towards the sea. I sat and gazed on the rains and allowed the image of Sylvia Doran, naked, to fall into a dark recess of my soul, allowed the voice of a quizzical God to become an echo from a far hill, allowed all turbulence to settle like sand after a storm.

Sometimes I walked over the headlands to fish for pollack off the rocks. I flung the bait out far and I drew it back in, slowly. I threw it out again and I drew it back in, slowly. Beyond the reach of the sea I dreamed of nothing, experiencing the indifference of salt wind on my face, the occasional tremor of excitement at a catch, the view on the horizon of a trawler returning to harbour. I spent evenings with Charlie in the Harbour Bar and drank porter. I drank the quicker because I had little to say to Charlie and he even less to say to me. It was easy to let the mind float on a black tide of near-oblivion. Around me the country, too, seemed to grind to a stop, its concerns small and dark and regular.

"McGinley!"

"Yes, sir."

"How, McGinley, would you recognise a Communist?"

"Would he be talking Russian, sir?"

"He would, McGinley, surely, or double Dutch to you. Never manage to get a pint in the Harbour Bar. Anything else, McGinley, to make you spot a Communist in the lanes of Carrickmore?"

"He wouldn't be going to Mass, sir."

"True, McGinley, true. But what if it was a Saturday afternoon, McGinley, how would you spot him then?"

"He might be shouting at the people that there's no God, sir, or getting them to start a revolution."

"In Carrickmore, McGinley?"

"Yes, sir. (A pause.) (Triumphantly:) And he wouldn't be going to Confession, sir."

In Carrickmore the history lessons were as simple as they had always been. The struggle of mother Ireland against the bully, England. And we have almost thrown him off, boys, almost thrown him off. He's riding our chest, boys, still sitting heavily on us, riding our chest. And, without the enthusiasm of Master Brosnan, I rattled off:

Oh the Erne shall run red
With redundance of blood,
The earth shall rock beneath our tread,
And flames wrap hill and wood,
And gun-peal and slogan cry
Wake many a glen serene,
Ere you shall fade, ere you shall die,
My Dark Rosaleen!

Many a glen serene! I tried to ignore the constant re-election of de Valera during those years; I tried to shrug all of that from my consciousness, walking to the quiet of my room, the heaving of the sea, the darkness of the Harbour Bar.

"Deeney!"

"Yes, sir."

"How would you know a Blueshirt, Deeney?"

"He'd be wearing a blue shirt, sir."

"Suppose he had a coat on, Deeney?"

Pause.

"He'd be at Mass on Sunday, sir."

"Suppose it was a Saturday afternoon, Deeney."

Pause.

"He'd be going on about the Communists, sir, and he'd be going to Confession."

"And would he be off to Spain on his holidays, Deeney?"

"No, sir, he'd be going to fight for Franco and for the Catholics and for the Pope, sir."

Good boy, Deeney. And when Deeney raced his dog along the slopes of Coolrea Hill, what mattered to him was the plumpness of sheep on the higher slopes, and the sweetness of the mutton on the Deeney table.

Sometimes the IRA spoke out for me; the heroes of my father's war were forced into the role of gangsters until we grew sick of the violence.

"McGarvey!"

"Yes, sir."

"What does de Valera tell you to be satisfied with?"

"A frugal comfort, sir."

"Correct, McGarvey. And during your hours of leisure, what things should you be engaged in?"

"The things of the spirit, sir."

"Excellent boy! And are you satisfied with your frugal comforts, McGarvey?"

" … "

"And do you devote your free time to the concerns of the spirit?"

" … "

Of course their fathers were the makers of bombs, the drivers of trucks on secret sorties, during their leisure hours, across the border on the darkest of nights.

"Dances, Madden, dances!"

"Dances, sir?"

"In the Starlight, Madden. Are they of God?"

"I don't know, sir."

"What did the Canon say at Mass on Sunday, Madden?"

"He said that dances was the work of the divil, sir."

"Not dances, Madden, be more accurate, boy, what did the Canon say?"

"He said close dancin', sir, touchin', like … "

"Good man, Madden, there you have it. Touchin'. A terrible thing, touchin'."

And they stared at me, and wondered. But my head was down, and my fists were only used to grasp a porter glass or a Wilkie Collins novel, and my body would sail along on its bike across the harmless hills and valleys of Donegal.

Charlie's imagination was a deeply Catholic one and the only area of imaginative excitement in those years was to tell of ghosts, devils, fairies, leprechauns, cloven hooves ... The mysteries of the Rosary dragged Charlie's imagination into realms of the fantastical and we would draw in around the hearth after the long addenda to the prayers, and chat in reverent tones of the dead and the near-dead, while Mrs B. made us all a nice, wholesome cup of hot cocoa.

"Did you ever hear tell of the big Man of Veel?" Charlie asked. The light from the lamp was a pale lemon behind us in the centre of the kitchen, the wind outside on the fields was cold and restless. It was a time for ghosts.

"No, Charlie, who was he?"

"Well, old Peter Turley was digging a trench up by the clump of stones they called the Monastery when he found this skellington lying in a shallow grave. He was seven foot tall, thin and long as a mast, buried without a stitch of cloth left to him or any trace of a coffin about him."

"Must have been during the famine, Charlie."

"Not at all, Matt, not at all. Several of the skellington's bones had been broken and the body, stretched out full, had its hands under its back and its two feet crossed at the ankles. Peter knew it was some kind of sign that the giant had either lived ay unnatural life or had died ay unnatural death."

Charlie eyed me shrewdly, and waited.

"There's more, Charlie?" I prodded.

"There is then!" he pronounced with satisfaction. "A good deal more. There was a skull found with him, down between his shin-bones. A skull, no more! Just a small, wee skull locked in beneath his twisted legs."

"And what's the explanation of it all, Charlie?"

"It's clear this giant murdered a child, probably by

cutting his head off. And when the terrible crime was discovered the giant was tied hands and feet and clubbed to death, and the skull of the child buried with him to be his accuser when we all come together at the latter end to be tried, rewarded and condemned. But what's the strangest of all? They took the skull and they took the skellington and they gave them separate graves up in Reily graveyard, destroying the eternal plan that would bring this murdered child some justice. And now, up on the headland at Turley's place, there's only a wild kind of emptiness where the ghost of this child wails and keens. It's cruel cold up in them fields and there's nobody has ever been able to grow a spud or a carrot up there, no and even the sheep and the donkeys won't graze on the grass because it's mad haunted. There's for you. It's a terrible thing to disturb the dead. There's them, too, that tell of the giant that haunts the western edge of Reily graveyard, his tall shape against the bare stone walls, his bones rattling as he tries to untangle them, his voice high and lost, like a curlew's cry over a sea in storm."

"Sounds like Eamon de Valera giving an election speech from the back of a lorry," I joked, but the blasphemy did not go well in the hushed atmosphere of the room.

"God almighty Matt but you must be the fierce horrid unbeliever, now, what?" challenged Charlie.

"Not at all, Charlie," I answered, "but there's always a reasonable explanation for things. I just simply do not believe in ghosts."

Charlie accused me of scepticism, paganism, communism, that I was an atheist, a rationalist, a sinner. Then he stopped, and added

"And a coward!"

I countered his stupidity with reasonable arguments, with my own experiences in the faith, not telling him, of course, of my recent years, adding there was nothing on this earth I feared. That's how the challenge came about.

There was a large abandoned house out on the road to Carrickmore. I passed the high piers of the gate every day on my bike; it was an old manor, deserted for years, the owners, so Charlie claimed, driven out by ghosts, the house built on the blood of murdered servants. Nobody ever went near the place now, never, ever.

"There's ghosts in that house, Matt, there's livin' ghosts in that house. And I'll put you now to the test … "

Would I sleep a night in that house? Of course I would. Alone? Certainly. Upstairs, in a bedroom? Why not? He would bet me five pounds I would not last the night!

"There must be no tricks, Charlie."

"No tricks, I swear it."

"You'll tell nobody about it?"

"I'll tell nobody, Matt, and anyway there's nobody that'd go next nor near the place."

"How will you know that I've spent the night?"

"I'll leave you at the gate in the evenin' and I'll call for you in the mornin' and I'll trust you on it."

"I'll take a gun, Charlie, my own point 22, and I'll use it, mind, if I suspect anyone is playing tricks on me. I'm a good shot, and I've a steady hand."

On the following Friday evening I brought blankets from my room, took my rifle and cartridges, candles and a box of matches. We began with a few whiskeys in the Harbour Bar. I bought a naggin and we staggered the noisy Ford out the three miles to the manor. I was scarcely out of the car before Charlie had turned and driven off, the sounds fading rapidly into the darkness about me.

Fool, I had yielded to the foolishness of a foolish man in a foolish time. The sycamores around the gate were loud in the breeze. It was cold and so dark I regretted not bringing a torch. I stood a while waiting for my eyes to gather shapes out of the darkness. Gradually the gate and the high piers outlined themselves. I tried the gate; it was impossible to shift. I pushed my blankets between the bars and climbed over, then made my way along the avenue, grasses, brambles, clutching at me, only the vague shapes and sounds of trees defining my path.

The house loomed, blackness against the lesser blackness of a clouded sky. I made my way round to the side, holding my body against the walls to guide myself. I reached the base of iron steps and began to climb, blindly, taking the greatest care. At times things breathed away above my head, their bat-flight intuited rather than heard. The old iron steps groaned and squeaked. I came onto a grill before French windows. There was little glass left, I stepped through and stood, watching onto the deepest darkness I had ever been aware of. I fumbled for a candle. Gradually the form of an empty room took shape. Apart from the double windows through which I had come, there was one further window facing the front of the house. The door at the far end of the room was closed and intact. There was a smell of damp and must, the stale odour of bird-shit and rotting timbers. I crossed the floor, like a ballet dancer, testing the beams. I chose a corner as far as possible from the drafts and laid out my blankets. I put my rifle, loaded, against the wall and stood the unstoppered whiskey bottle, allowing its rich and heady scent to tickle the ugliness of the room. Then I made my way to the door onto the landing.

I held the candle in my left hand; the knob of the door was loose but it turned; there was a key on the inside but the door was not locked. I opened it slowly. Beyond, there was darkness. I stepped out to see the landing and found an abyss before me; I dropped the candle in shock and it fell into that blackness and went out; I grabbed for the jamb of the door and saved myself from falling after the candle. It was a lucky escape. I got my second candle and, lying flat on my stomach, edged myself back over the threshold; slowly the extent of that hole revealed itself; there was no landing, no stairway, no banisters, just space, jagged beams of wood, the ceiling and roof above had caved in, too. Beneath there was a hell of slates and plaster, wooden beams and dust. The house was a cluster of rooms about a void where the rain and wind were the sole inhabitants. I thanked God for my escape and felt no kindness towards Charlie.

I went back into the room, closed the door and began to settle into the foolishness of the night. It was cold but several gulps from the whiskey bottle and a careful wrapping of myself in blankets had me feeling benevolent towards the living and the dead. I stood the candle beside me; the gentle light burned steadily.

I slept. And woke suddenly. Something had reached into my sleep and touched me. The candle still burned but there was only a little of it left. I took out my watch, opened it and held the face near the flame. Three-thirty. I shivered; it was very, very cold. The wind seemed to have died away completely. The silence was as hard as ice.

When I heard footsteps mounting the stairs outside the room the world stopped for me from its perpetual, slow, circling; my life stopped, my breathing, my heart, and I existed for a while in a vacuum of fear as cold as the deepest hole of space must be. There was no staircase outside! yet there was somebody coming up the stairs, stepping loudly, with definite purpose. A shivering began in my hair, somewhere behind my ears, and spread rapidly, chilling my hands to the fingertips; my stomach knew a sudden hollowness that was distressing. The inside of my brain was a violent scarlet colour as if a scream of terror raced round and round within it and was unable to escape. And still the footsteps, inexorably. My eyes were fixed on the door, on that round, loose knob and I knew that soon it would begin to turn and I would no longer be able to live.

The footsteps stopped outside. I could not move. There was silence. Suddenly the candle beside me guttered and went out. I screamed, then, I screamed, my whole body gathering in a paroxysm of chilled terror around that scream; I closed my eyes, I was going to die, I did not want to live, I was a fool, a fool and I was lost.

I do not know how long I screamed. When I quietened down I was aware that everything around me had returned to silence. I could hear my own breathing, its great gasps, its sobbing, I could feel the battering of my heart and that thumping pain high in my chest. I reached for the third candle, and after several attempts, my hands trembling so, succeeded in lighting it. I watched towards the door. It remained closed. There was silence beyond.

I took a great slug of whiskey and it braced me, quickly. With determination I got up, picked up the candle and went softly to the door. I don't know where the courage, or the foolhardiness came from, but I opened that door onto my fear. There was nothing but emptiness and darkness and the feeble light of my candle made no impression on that eternity. My body was cold as if it had been immersed for hours in the icy sea, and every bit of my flesh was shivering. I closed the door then, and turned the key, realising as I did so the foolishness of my action. I went back to my hiding-place and tried to warm myself with whiskey. The silence was full again, untrusted.

I knew that soon, inevitably, the world's wheeling would be perceptible again and a glimmering of daylight would call to me from the windows. I took out my watch; scarcely two minutes had gone by. I placed the watch, opened, beside the candle. I reached out and touched the solid presence of the rifle, I handled the cartridges, too, and their firm individual presences were soothing to my fingers. How foolish is the mind of man.

The pounding pain in my chest had not been there for a long time but now it was agonising. Perhaps it was the sudden return of that pain that had felt like the footsteps of horror coming up the steps outside my body. The thought gave my mind some relief, but brought none to my body. I breathed hard to try and ease the pain, remembering that soldier, his hatred, his bitterness.

I grew aware once again that the footsteps were mounting that non-existent staircase outside. Oh that same chilled and chilling trembling took me and I jerked upright in a spasm of terror. Slow, heavy, inevitable tread, up, up, up, from what awful depths of horror or non-being? I was bent forward with the agony of my fear and still I could not move. And then, then, impossible, insupportable! the knob on the door of my room began to turn, the footsteps became a slow shuffling just outside, and that old, erratic knob moved slowly. There was a pause, and then the door was shaken. I looked towards the key. Can a locked door keep such terrors out? The knob was turned again, and again, and then the door was shaken more violently. I moved.

"Who's there?" I screamed and the scream was no release to me.

There was only silence as an answer. The knob turned again. I screamed again.

"Who's there? Is there anybody there?"

I imagined the old frail bones of the house shaken under the panic of my screaming as if moths of dust came loose from a million million tiny insects disturbed and flying into the night. There was only silence as an answer.

It came to me then, touching my stammering mind, that one of Charlie's friends was out there, that there were several of them out there, giggling to themselves, rehearsing the mockery they would shower on me from here on out.

"I have a gun!" I shouted. "Charlie knows I have a gun and I will use it!"

Silence.

I heard a shuffling noise again and then those same slow, heavy footsteps went down the non-existent stairs. I reached for the rifle and put the extra cartridges in my jacket pocket. I let off the safety catch, cocked the gun and raised it towards the door. I waited. A long time. Perhaps a minute. Perhaps five. The rifle grew heavy in my hands and I let the barrel droop. But I was ready. One more warning, then I would shoot.

I was not surprised when the footsteps began again. Up, up that staircase, out of the chaos down below. Clump, clump, clump, regular, awful, determined. Somehow I knew it was not Charlie, nor any of Charlie's friends, the sounds were not real, and they were too real. That shuffling sound again from just beyond the door.

"Stop!" I screamed. "Stop. I will shoot!"

I raised the barrel but it was heavy as death and trembled hopelessly in my hands. The rattling of the door persisted. I pulled the rifle stock hard in against my shoulder, aimed as best I could towards the lower part of the door and pulled the trigger. The sound of the explosion was violent in the confined spaces of my terror but the bullet missed the door and made a great rent low in the wall to the right.

I managed to eject the spent cartridge and insert another although my hands trembled and fumbled. I took a deep breath and my father's words came out of the safe and warm places of my soul. "When you aim ... "

More steadily I raised the gun again and aimed, trying to follow the words. I aimed for the groin of the door, I fired. The bullet went through the door as cleanly as a thought. The rattling continued. I took the rifle by the barrel and flung it against the door. Then I sat down in my corner to wait. I was crying. I waited.

The rattling stopped. I waited. I heard shuffling noises. Then a loud rush and a great thump against the door so that it shook in its frame. I was crying aloud, now, wailing, there was another rush and a thud against the door. The door held. But there was a splintering sound and I screamed.

"Jesus! Jesus! Jesus!" over and over until I realised that once again there was silence. I reached into my pocket and drew out the rosary that I had bought to please Mrs Blackshaw. The feel of the crucified figure brought relief as did the speaking of the prayers into the darkness and the slow, fretful fingering of the beads. There was silence from beyond. I glanced at the watch. It was a quarter to four. Soon, there would be light. I prayed, going round that small circle of eternity within the compass of my hands, finding comfort, relishing the silence yet dreading a reoccurrence of those footsteps.

The seconds were hours long, the minutes days. At four thirty the great wooden frame of the window in the front of the house began to take shape. I got up, cautiously, retrieved my rifle, backed slowly onto the grid outside the windows. The blankets lay huddled like a dead person on the floor; the small light of the candle burned on. I looked towards the door with the bullet-hole clean through it and then backed carefully down the iron steps. Daylight was faint but I could see my way; I backed down the avenue to the iron gate, my eyes fixed on the ugly, blank holes of the upstairs windows, the great bulk of the blinded, heartless house. I prayed, holding my crucifix tightly. I climbed the gate and was back on the road to Killybegs. The road stretched ahead of me, a faint grey through the brown darkness of dawn. I walked as quickly as my hurt mind and weary body would allow, looking back over my shoulder, often and often, the sense of dread fading slowly. The first sound of bird-song startled me. And then I sat down on a low stone wall and cried, my head in my hands, I cried for the frailty of our living, for the helplessness of our unknowing.

The snake that went round and round forever, trying to swallow its own tail. Worlds beyond our world and we have only the faintest intimations. The broken, ugly and pathetic body of the Christ, I can touch with my own bruised fingers. That broken figure is all there is or ever has been between me and my death. I woke Charlie out of his deep, comfortable sleep and put a five pound note into his fist. I said nothing. When he opened his eyes from the morning fog that was in them and looked at me, he did not need to say anything either.

DAVID

You came into the game
from a starting-point near rocks
and ran, trying to reach the stone
placed at the centre, the den, the safehouse, home;

and there I go –
screaming round the outermost circle,
father pounding after,
a switch of sea-wrack in his hand.

Eternity, he told me, is like the letter O,
it has no beginning and no end,
or like the nought, perhaps,
and you could slither down and down

through its black centre.
With a silver pin
he drew the periwinkles from their shells,
soft flesh uncoiling from the whorl;

he scooped out gravelly meat from the barnacle,
swallowed its roundness whole, with that black
mucous-like blob at its centre;
and there I go, half nauseated,

following;
the way you become your father,
that same diffidence and turning inwards,
that same curving of the spine,

the way the left shoulder lifts in emphasis;
and here I am,
pounding round the outermost circle,
a switch of sea-wrack in my hand.

MATTHEW

I TOOK MY RIFLE WITH ME WHEN I WENT FISHING, OR DOWN THE
rocks along the edge of the coast, searching for solitude. I
felt a growing urge to lift the rifle, aim and fire, to know I
had hit something with precision. I would stop in my
fishing, leave down the rod, pick up the rifle, aim at a
gannet far out over the sea. I would focus, flying with the
bird, soaring, diving, knowing the secret of its living, and
then I would pull the trigger, gently, a soft, loving touch.

On such occasions I did not have the gun loaded.
Except once. I saw a cormorant sweeping around the
headland, holding its course barely a foot above the water,
flying at speed, a black arrow, ignorant of me, vanishing
for moments in the waves, wing-tips touching the surface
of the sea. Something touched me to anger. I loaded,
aimed, followed its flight a while, then touched the trigger.

The bird crashed into the water at once, as if it had hit
the hard, invisible wall of eternity. I was astonished at
myself; the heron that had risen over the woods at the
Glenshale Pass only to be shot into foolishness by the
soldier, came into my mind and I was ashamed, angry with
myself, angry with the sea that carried to my feet the mess
of the black-feathered, burst-open body.

I loved the feel of the cartridge belt about me; I loved
the sleeved perfection of each cartridge in its pouch, that
golden roundness catching the sun, how each cartridge
slipped from its pouch and slotted, perfect as a
mathematical solution, into the breach. I loved the solid

weight of the rifle on my shoulder, its companionship, the smooth hardness of the stock. And when I cleaned it out, pulling a cord through the barrel with a piece of linen attached, that hold and sudden yield as I pulled, that smooth, cleansing journey back into the air. I would aim at the heart of a rock, sound a "Pachow!" in a whisper, aim at a cloud, or a tree, happy in it, filling my solitude with dreams.

I joined Charlie in his empty silences, the way he would lean his head over the bar, his big fisherman's fists around his pint. Germany was the word we heard, something menacing out there across miles of land and sea, something big and threatening, like a bully. Around us de Valera was creating martyrs with his Offences Against the State Act and his Emergency Powers Act. In the darkness of the Harbour Bar I tried to keep a distance between myself and that world. That bloodlust.

Charlie sighed deeply.

"Bothering you, Charlie?"

"It's this war, Matt, has me thinkin'. It's this war."

"War's a terrible thing, Charlie, terrible, and you'd think we've learned enough about wars over the centuries never to go to war again."

"It's not that, Matt, not that at all."

"What is it, Charlie?"

"There's talk about the boats, Matt. They say it won't be safe to go to our own fishing grounds fairly soon."

"I didn't hear that, Charlie."

"There's no future for me here, Matt. The fishing's a desperate hard game and there's little reward for it but cold and fish-scales and fish-shit. And with this war … "

"What are you thinking of, Charlie?"

"I'm for England, Matt, next week I'm for England. I'm goin' to join up, maybe there's a future out there."

He spoke with a determination that allowed no space

for challenge, gesturing vaguely beyond the cobwebbed window of the Harbour Bar.

Late that night the storm broke, coming in slowly from the Atlantic. At first, as we walked home, a different Charlie beside me, in the distant rumbling you could imagine artillery firing. And we saw several crackles of fire on the horizon as if the very limits of our world had split open, allowing glimpses of the terrifying wall of light beyond. He closed the hall door behind us. The house was still. As we turned to go upstairs I touched him gently on the shoulder in a good-night and he jumped from me, startled, as if I no longer existed in his world.

I could not sleep. The power of the storm approached slowly. I left the curtains undrawn. Light and darkness alternated in the room. The blank ceiling became a wall, dull and flat and uninspiring and I was pressed against it, like a deserter about to be shot. I got up, dressed, and went out into the storm. It had not yet begun to rain but a wind was growing and the shifting darknesses of the storm-clouds tumbled overhead. I made my way down to the strand. The sea had risen and great waves were washing towards the land. In the otherworldly light I walked the jagged edge left by the last wave. The whole force of the storm seemed to gather over this stretch of coast, over this strand. The thunder was about my head, great thuds of drums and the slowly receding tympani of sound, the almost instant flash of lightning that lit the world with a curious silver precision, as seeming-solid to the touch as the track left by a snail.

The rain came, at once drenching and intense. I stood and gazed north into the storm and the sea and allowed the whole force of nature to probe and chasten me. I was no Lear standing proud and self-righteous against mankind, I was but a solitary man faced once again with the burden of his own uncertain being. I had come to lean so much on that one, big foolish fisherman; I had come to rely on the dunes, the dips and hollows of this northern hide-away. I had come to stand on the creaking turf-cart of my Catholic belief, I had fallen foul of this world and of the next, I was an eel, twisting upon itself in a jam-jar filled with stagnant water.

The rains washed over me with a violence I had not known before. The sea came about my shoes and washed and gripped at my feet. I raised my hands and took the storm and washed my face with it, rubbing and rubbing until I felt I could get the cleansing power through into my brain. I would begin again. It was the end of another day. I had seen a vacancy in a school in the west, in Achill island. Perhaps I could leave my ghosts behind me. Morning and night. Another dawning. Another place.

Six

David

Love

is like starting on a pilgrimage,
stepping blithely out over the gunwale
hoping to waltz on water;

hands working inside one another's lives,
grasping the heart, for hold.
I heard their voices through the wall

like summer murmuring;
he brought her honeycombs
in wooden frames soft as the host,

a small, hard ball of wax
stayed forever in her mouth
after the sweetness.

But in the photograph they are still
striding out together along the beach,
smiling, confident,

striding into the confusion
of their final months, their love
a bonding, dulled, unspoken,

they will disappear, exemplary, together
as if the sea had swallowed them,
leave echoes of a low, ongoing, music.

MATTHEW

I HAD THOUGHT LOVE WOULD COME THE WAY HIS GOD HAD COME
to Saul on the road, flinging him suddenly onto the earth,
blinding him with certainty. I had expected it to hit with an
anvil-ding and with fire. But it came, stealing as spring
through me, melting me, mastering me, too; it was, as
Hopkins wrote, a lingering-out sweet skill.

She was a teacher, like me, in a small, two-roomed
building with high partitions and a sea-wind perpetually
chalking its marks along the walls. I taught in a school
many miles away, down a pathway covered with sand, the
village lying low between me and the Church, the
schoolyard filled all afternoon with the cries of gulls
foraging for the crumbs from the boys' lunches, filled all
morning, until the long, slow molten-gold notes of the
Angelus bell dropped from the sky onto the unfenced
fields. We discovered one another at a meeting of the
elders of the island, doctors, chemists, priests, hoteliers,
teachers, to discuss the drawbacks of the Emergency and to
establish some social life to drive the ghosts away.

We stood in the hall, drinking precious tea out of flasks
the hoteliers had provided. Outside the rains were wild
herds circling the hall, drummers banging their finger-tips
across the galvanised roof.

I was at ease with her, and after the meeting we chatted
on about the schools, and teaching, and the words came
easily to me, it seemed as if I'd known Joanne all my life.
We went out then into the evening. There was a soft light

still on the horizon; the night was still and warm. We spoke quietly, and I did not want our meeting to stop. I walked her home and we stood at the gate to her house, and there was a warmth between us that was precious to me. At last, as she turned to go in, I reached high and picked a small branch alive with white hawthorn blossoms and offered it to her. She laughed and accepted it. I felt as if I had leaped into the sky and caught a fistful of stars.

We met then, often, and very soon she knew all about my life and I knew about hers. We walked the island together, the roads, the strands, the mountain slopes. And after a few weeks I knew she had slipped into my life so deeply that it would hurt beyond measure should I lose her. Joanne put order on the crude circling of the world. Perhaps the place we strive to find is not a locus, but a state of love. She conquered my restlessness because she was there, she overcame my hesitations because she did not insist.

How the heart, being buoyant, can float over the turgid stream of foolishness. We were in love, Joanne and I, around us the island of Achill lay in the pride of its wildering beauty and muscular power, God was in His Heaven, and I was at home.

Jack McHugh came one grey summer afternoon and when I drove up to the gate of our house he was standing there, his son Padraig with him, agitation in every inch of his body. Jack was a small farmer who lived in the village and his family had always been good friends to Joanne's family and now to us.

"Ah, Matt!" he rushed, as soon as I had stepped out of the car; "Matt, I have a great favour to ask of you."

"Go ahead, Jack, ask."

"It's the mare, Matt, she's after breaking her right foreleg on me and I'm afraid she's finished. We'll have to put her down."

"I'm sorry to hear that, Jack," I said, "but I'm no vet."

"Ah no, and we have no time to fetch the vet. They say you can shoot the eye out of a magpie from a hundred yards, Matt!"

"So you think I could hit a horse, with luck!"

"Well, I'll tell you now. I'm very fond of the poor old beast, and I want her to slide out of the world like shit out of a goose, if you'll pardon the expression."

"I'll pardon you, Jack, but I'm not following you."

"No pain, Matt, no suffering, no indignity. Clean."

"Like shit out of a goose?"

We went out at once, Jack and I, he bringing his son with him, I bringing mine. Two cartridges only I brought, in the pocket of my waistcoat, the gun resting gentle as a dance-partner on my arm. We walked back to the bog near Loughnaneaneen. There the mare waited, with two men, two neighbours. They had dug a deep hole in the wet bogland, the sides sliced neat and clean and brown, the bottom filled with peaty water. Jack manoeuvred the old mare until she was standing at the edge of the hole, her hoof hanging like a broken branch. All about us was waste moorland, hillocks, tussocks, an occasional bog-deal root. In the near distance rose the slopes of Mweelin Mountain, above us the vast sky over Achill. There were clouds, grey and almost motionless.

I put the first cartridge in the gun. The eye of the mare was big and calm, as if she knew her strange hour had come at last. I moved about ten yards from her. The two men had moved back; only Jack stood with the mare, whispering to her, rubbing her neck with evident sorrow. The tail swished gently. At last Jack turned and nodded, the plea in his face almost more than I could bear. He moved away a few feet and stood, facing her. I raised the rifle and aimed.

I had shot rabbits on the island, relished the alert innocence of them as they moved among the sand-dunes of the Valley; I had shot the wild geese and duck as they muttered in their foreign tongues among the reeds, shifting in their little congregations at dusk, or floating in colourful convoys on the surface of the lake. Always I had relished that trigger touch, the power the soft flesh of my finger against the grey coldness of the trigger never failed to offer.

Now as I aimed, the instinct was still there. My hands were steady, my body stilled, the small area behind the mare's eye in my sights. "When you aim ... " But there was that resignation in the eye of the mare, that awful loss that made Jack McHugh's large body sag as if a spring had been broken inside him, I could master no strength to pull the trigger. The silence deepened. The expectation was palpable. I lowered the rifle.

Nobody spoke. If there had even been one breath of wind to upset the silence ... The mare's tail swished patiently. I sighed. And then I saw my son, frightened, eager, his young eyes fixed on me in expectation. How can we know what image of ourselves comes in, like a wild duck, to settle in our children's minds? I deliberately conjured up the memory of the soldier standing in the yard, ready to thud his rifle butt into my chest; I recalled the soldiers racing down the hill while my father was unable to move after the train. Quickly then I turned, raised the rifle, and fired.

The afternoon seemed to split apart at the sound, as a boulder splits from the dynamite that has been living and hatching at its heart. The echoes were hoarse screams rushing about and trying to escape, into the bog, into the lake, into the mountain, into the sky. I lowered the rifle. The mare seemed unaffected. She stood, that great eye wide open, startled as we all were. I began to wonder if the bullet had missed her completely and had flown off into the distance. Then, slowly, very slowly, she began to keel over, the way a tree falls, stiffly, upright and dignified until the last moment.

Jack went up to the hole and looked in. Then he turned and came to where I stood.

"Perfect!" he said and there were tears in his eyes. "Perfect!"

He shook me by the hand. We could say no more. I turned away and my own son took my hand and held it and walked proudly with me, without speaking, back to our own place.

DAVID

WE STOOD TOGETHER AT ACHILL SOUND, MOTHER, FATHER AND I, during the excitement of a fair day. We were in the open space behind the shops where there were stalls erected, selling all sorts of things, clothes, wellington boots, games, holy pictures, sweets. There were cows and donkeys and a few horses at one end of the fair ground, small gatherings of men at each others' pockets. A lorry drew up into the area, parked parallel to the wall behind the shops. Several men got out and began to organise loudspeakers from the high ends of the lorry.

They began to play music and collected the attention of everybody present. Father and Mother seemed excited. Somebody mentioned the name of Eamon de Valera and I remember how Mother took Father's hand in hers and held it very tightly. Then a tall, dignified, elderly man came out of a car that had been waiting, unnoticed in a corner of the fair ground. Eamon de Valera. He was very tall and wore thick lenses on his glasses. He was helped up onto the back of the lorry and stood at the microphone, waiting.

A buzz of excitement went round among the people and the music died. The crowds gathered round when they saw who it was and I stood beside my parents close to the side of the lorry. We looked up and he was there above us, his hands thrust deep into the pockets of a big, black coat, his face gaunt and serious, a dull light off his round glasses. My father was tense and very quiet and I know he must have been pleased to have come so close to the great man.

I cannot remember anything at all that de Valera said that day, from the back of the old red lorry, in the fairgreen of Achill Sound. Once Father lifted me up so that I could get a better look but he put me down again, saying I was getting too heavy for him.

Then, from somewhere, a voice screamed something at the man in the lorry and de Valera hesitated, surprised. From somewhere else something flew towards him and hit the roof of the lorry cab. De Valera drew himself up, and continued to speak. A murmuring had begun among the crowd and I could see my father growing more and more tense. He gathered me closely to him, in his shelter, and moved back a little from the lorry. Again he took Mother's hand and they drew very close together.

Suddenly something broke against de Valera's long overcoat and spread out in an ugly stain; someone had thrown an egg. There was a cheer from the crowd and at once other things were being flung at the lorry. De Valera was helped down and several policemen moved between the crowd and the lorry. The great man was bundled into the car and driven quickly away from the fair green.

"That's terrible!" Father was saying, "terrible! No matter what you think of a man you must give him a chance to speak. Violence has never solved anything, never, never, never, and it never will."

I thought of the smail classroom where Father spent so much of his life and I began to fear for him, that he had not lived, that he had never come close to the great waves that rise in the history of the world. I noticed a rip in the pocket of his jacket, a small rent where the stitching had come loose; and for a moment I was ashamed of his smallness, of the pettiness of his life, of his failure.

MATTHEW

I WATCHED THEM DIG GREAT HOLES IN OUR FIELDS; THEY LEFT
poles in the ground, a straight line stretching out of
emptiness like a procession of beggarmen, across meadows
and ditches, over hedgerows and into the field behind the
house. I watched others come and climb those poles,
wearing extraordinary shoes, like snowshoes, great hooks
at the toe. They lay back against the wind and fitted perfect
tulip-flowers to the small crossbeams on top. Later big
lorries came and unloaded spools large as steam-roller
wheels; they unrolled the wires and attached them,
stitching the island of Achill to the world beyond.

That evening we put away the delicately-wrought magic
lamps that had been our light forever, and got ready to
turn on the electricity for the very first time. We stood in
the porch, the front door opening on to dusk, waiting for
the moment. The front gate was opened by a strange
figure. He strode confidently up the path. He came with
such silence and suddenness out of the gloom that my
chest pounded suddenly with his coming. He called out:

"Matt?"

You circle, year after year after year, struggling to come
to terms with life, thinking you have found the answer,
losing it and taking up the search again. Always knowing,
somewhere deep within, there will come a moment, a
person or an event that will shape the most important
point on the circle of your life.

I knew the voice at once though the body seemed

heavier and more leaden than the years should have taken toll of. I reached out and grasped his hand and his clasp was strong and firm as ever.

"Manus Cafferky! is it you? and where on God's earth did you spring from?"

Just then we could see the lights coming on in the houses round our townland. Joanne looked at me expectantly and touched the switch; a fine, white light lit up the porch, the front steps, and reached out along the garden path. We cheered, and we could hear the sounds of cheering from the other houses.

"So!" Manus said, "I come like the angel, bringing light!"

He would not come into the house, he said he would be leaving the island almost at once. He drew me down the path, out onto the road and we walked through the silence of the evening. He was living in Monaghan, he told me, builder's labourer. No, he had never married; there had been Delia … For almost an hour we went over our lives, rehearsing our movements, our circling, our hopes, finally agreeing that we each, at last, had found our place.

"Now, Matt," and he stopped and faced me; it was not easy to make out his features in the darkness. "There's a very special task we want you to perform."

"We? Manus, who're we?"

"I'm talking about the IRA, Matt."

He went on to tell me about the struggle, how he had sworn his life to a united Ireland, how he had worked and fought, going underground when de Valera declared them illegal, how he had spent seven years in custody in the Curragh, how they saw de Valera as the great blight on the horizon of their hopes.

"That's a turn-about," I said, "from the time you and I fought in St Joseph's … "

"You're not too fond of de Valera yourself, Matt?"

"No, Manus, I'm not fond of him, not one little bit."

"We have this special task, Matt, for you … "

It was now quite dark, the great sky over Achill black and starless, only the lights from the houses bringing a little comfort and definition to the place. Manus had come, he said, with a mandate from the leadership of the IRA, to me, because they wanted this job done by someone wholly unknown to the authorities, on whom no possible suspicion could fall, while they themselves would have alibis when the deed was done.

"Deed, Manus? What are you talking about?"

"About you, Matt, about you. An assassination, Matt. That's what we're talking about."

The words fell on the ground before me, flat and dull as stones. I could not see Manus's eyes, only a faint outline of his shape before me. Gradually the words began to take on some semblance of meaning. I laughed.

"That's ridiculous, Manus, you don't think I'm just going to get my gun and shoot Eamon de Valera, do you?"

"Matt, that is precisely what you are going to do." His voice was low and steady, full of certainty and insistence. "There's a celebration of some sort taking place in Rockwell College next week and de Valera will be there. He taught there once, you know, mathematics or something. And he's to give a speech from a platform in the grounds. A speech about nothing. Not important. Only about Rockwell and the Holy Ghost Fathers and the wonders of the Catholic Faith. So that nobody will be expecting anything. And the security will be lazy. And we hear you're nifty with a rifle … "

I could not believe what I was hearing. Now the deep darkness of the Achill night was growing oppressive. The presence of this man brought something of enormous rottenness into the purity of my life.

"Manus," I sad, beginning to turn from him, "you had better be getting on your way. You had better say no more!"

He caught my arm out of the darkness.

"Oh, no, Matt, no," he said and his voice now was vile, seething with determination. "This is something you have to do. We have decided on you, and now you know what our thoughts are and what we intend, we cannot let you not do it. The Man insists. It's an order, Matt, not a request."

I jerked my arm from his grasp.

"I don't take orders from the IRA, from The Man, whoever he is, or from you, Manus."

"Oh but you do, Matt, you do. Do you think we didn't expect you might refuse? Your son, now, what's this his name is, ah yes, David, that's it, isn't it? What age is he now? six, seven, ten? and he's in school, isn't he? Oh yes and every afternoon he goes out the road to meet you, doesn't he?"

"You bastard!" I said, "don't involve him in this!"

"It's up to you, Matt, up to you, and when you go home now just look in his schoolbag, Matt, and see the little gift we gave him. OK, just a book this time, just a book. This time. Don't blame him, how could he know? One of our people gave it to him when he was coming home from school, told him to put it in his bag, that he'd be needing it for school later on. He's young, Matt. A fine boy. He took the little gift. Could have been a bomb, Matt, it could have been a bomb!"

I reached out of the darkness and struck at him. But he had anticipated it and he stepped back. Then, as if he could see through that blackness, he grasped my wrists with awful strength and held me.

"Matt, you have no way out of this. You must do it or your son will suffer an accident. You will rid our country of the great liar who has poisoned our lives. You will drive to Westport, park your car at a place we'll tell you. There you will wait until another car comes up behind you. You will get out, lock your own car, and will be given the keys to this new one. You will drive to Rockwell College and hide yourself and your rifle in the woods. In the car you will find food, blankets, a flask. Have a good night's sleep in the woods, Matt, nobody will be allowed into the grounds on Saturday. Take up your position where you can get a clear shot at the platform. De Valera will make his speech at noon. One shot, Matt, no trouble to you. Then get out! Back to the road, where our man will be waiting to take you home. Simple. Effective. No possible suspicion, Matt. Friday, after school. And remember, we know it all, your son, Joanne, we can reach them. Do it, Matt. It's what you were born for. Seven o'clock, Friday, at the quays, in Westport. Be there."

The last two words were spat at me and at once he dropped my wrists and moved into the darkness. I called out after him, but he had gone, so quickly he could have been a part of the blackness of the night. For over an hour I paced up and down outside the front gate of my house. When I went in I looked at once for David's schoolbag. I opened it and there, between his catechism and his table book, was a copy of "Irish History Reader." I took it out, my hands trembling; one of the pages was turned down at the top right-hand corner, the words underlined in red ink; *"Irishmen, claiming the right to make their own laws, should never rest content until their native Parliament is restored; and that Ireland looks to them, when grown to man's estate, to act the part of true men in furthering the sacred cause of nationhood."* Joanne was sitting by the fire, watching me. I took the book and closed David's bag. It was a small bag, brown leather, with cream stitching all around the edges, two small strips held by shining buckles. I caressed it, clumsily, with one hand. When I sat down by the fire opposite Joanne, I could not speak. My eyes filled with tears and she moved quickly to hold me.

"He's evil, Matt, isn't he?" was all she said.

I held her back from me and looked into her eyes.

Then I took the copy of "Irish History Reader" and threw it into the heart of the fire.

"Joanne, there is something I must do ... "

I drove out from Westport and took the road towards Luisburg. I came round the steep corner outside the town and drove down along the quays. There were several trawlers moored along the walls of the harbour. I drew my car in on the grassy patch at the end of the quay. It was six fifty, Friday evening. I sat and waited. Away to my left I could see the great bulk of Croagh Patrick rising against the darkness. There was a numbness in my body ever since Manus's visit and I moved without thought, dulled and deadened.

At five after seven a black Ford Prefect drew in behind me. I watched in the mirror as a man got out. He came up to my car and I rolled down the window. He dropped a key into my hand, then opened the door and held it open. I could not see his face. He looked around the quayside carefully; there was nobody about. I could hear the sea beat softly against the quay walls. I got out and locked the door of my car. The man followed me around to the boot; I opened it; my rifle was carefully wrapped up in its canvas sheathe. I lifted it out and closed down the lid of the boot. He held out his hand. I dropped the key of my car into it. He got in and drove away slowly, back towards the town.

It was after two o-clock when I drove into the yard of the hotel in Cahir. I waited. Soon a man appeared from the trees near the edge of the park. I gave him the key and we drove the few miles to Rockwell College. The headlights of the car lit up the great gates momentarily on our left; he allowed the car to coast gently down the hill, some sixty yards beyond the gate; then he turned to me.

"Here!" he said. "Five past twelve tomorrow."

When I had taken my rifle out of the boot, blankets, a flask, a brown paper package containing sandwiches, some biscuits, he drove away, the tail lights vanishing into the darkness back along the road towards Cahir. Then there was silence.

There were no stars and it was very cold. I could see sufficiently to make my way over a fence and in among trees. It was fragrant in the wood, soft underfoot, and I bumped and jostled my way along, as a blind man would. I knew that if I shot de Valera I would become a hero to many and to others I would be dirt. I remembered Kevin Barry, I remembered the day I tried to manipulate my life by yielding to the bloodlust and falling off my bicycle. I laughed. Innocent! and clever, too. Perhaps this was to be the floor of my greatness, perhaps it was for this I had been born. But I would not run from justice. Life would be over for me after such a crime; I would do my penance, whatever way my country judged me. And I would offer the name of Manus Cafferky so that some of my persecution would be avenged.

I came out at the edge of the trees; up on a low hill not far away was the huge shape of the college, lying like a great animal in its sleep, the high chimneys, turrets, outlined against the black of the night. There were no lights. Between me and the building were open spaces. I moved back from the edge of the wood and felt for a higher, dry spot to rest on. I spread my blankets in the darkness and sat on them, my back resting against a tree. How had I come to this … ?

The night was long. I did not sleep. I did not attempt to sleep. I wondered if the ghosts were here, all those ghosts that had haunted me over the years; now I had no fear of them. I stayed perfectly still among the trees; there was an occasional rustling and stirring in the undergrowth near me, an occasional whispering among the high branches of the trees; nothing more. On my heart a great sorrow, in my mind a growing clarity and determination.

I was cold. I drained the flask of tea mixed with whiskey that they had given me. I spoke with my father, with my mother and with Delia. And I spoke across the awful distance that had come between Joanne and me.

Dawn on that Saturday began about six o'clock. I stood and tried to ease the coldness and aching out of my body. I walked rapidly among the trees, swinging my arms, feeling numb as those tall companions of my vigil. Between me and the brown walls of the college were playing fields and a large stretch of meadow; a morning mist lay on everything and gradually, as I watched, it began to dissipate. It left the earth damp and cold and sparkling. By eight o'clock, when I could hear sounds from the college, I was searching for a vantage-point. The white painted timbers of a platform stood perhaps one hundred yards from the point I chose, a spot where the edge of the wood rose into a hillock and where there was a dense covering of escallonia bushes. I set the rifle up on the Y of branches where it rested perfectly, its mouth invisible from outside. I took out the one cartridge I had brought with me, its red covering the colour of blood, the golden end rounded to perfection. I opened the gun and loaded the cartridge. I gathered the blankets from the ground and wrapped them round me. I had some hours to wait.

Suddenly there was a tall, solitary figure walking slowly from the far end of the playing fields out into the day. He was wearing a dark suit. He was holding a walking-stick. To my astonishment, Eamon de Valera was walking clumsily in my direction. Alone.

He skirted the playing field, following a narrow cinder track that passed immediately in front of where I waited. At the speed at which he was walking he would pass, in a matter of minutes, less than a yard from the open mouth of the rifle. My heart began to pound sickeningly and my mouth went completely dry. I held the wooden butt of the rifle and my hands trembled. And there, once again, with its full ferocity, was that aching pain high up in my chest. I moved quietly to my left and had de Valera instantly in my sights.

He was taller than I had imagined him to be. He walked erect, his head high; he wore a black hat like a priest's, his glasses were rimless, the lenses round and thick. His suit was dark grey, the trousers baggy and unpressed, he wore a collarless shirt open at the neck. There was nobody else around. I could escape quickly through the trees, ignoring my noon meeting-time, and begin to work my way across Ireland towards the west. My excitement increased. I felt as if the trembling in my hands and the aching and pounding within my chest must be audible to the approaching man. I tried to calm myself. The gun rested easily on the branches, the butt firm, the barrel steady. This was to be my moment, then, my place in history, but it would remain, for ever, a secret, known only to a very few.

When he was about thirty yards from me de Valera paused and turned his head towards the trees. Could he have heard something? Very quietly I took off the safety catch and my finger moved to the trigger. From the way the big man cocked his head I knew he was listening for something; then I heard it, too, the high concerto of a wren from somewhere deep within the wood behind me. I noticed how his face fell into deep ridges of flesh behind his mouth when he smiled, how his eyes closed fully. Then he tensed again and continued towards me, his stick poking into the loose stones and cinders of the track ahead of him. He was twenty yards from me when I realised why his walk was an uneasy one, uncertain, broken in rhythm. The stick was an arm he used to grope his way forward.

He was almost blind, this man who had arrogantly set himself up as the conscience and soul of my country and had cajoled and pushed the people into following where he led, was ... blind! He was helpless before me.

For a long moment I came alive as I had never been before. Every individual leaf on the escallonia bush was clear, unique and beautiful, the sheen of its green a light in darkness, the pink bells of its flowers waiting to chime; even the smallest twig, in its brittleness, its jagged edges, seemed wondrous in its individuality. For that moment the whole chaos of the universe, its darknesses and its terrors, the miserable lot of human beings groping through their errors, their isolation and their untruths, the whole wheeling of our days and nights, our failure in integrity, the recurring nightmares of our wars, came together in my mind, concentrated on the tiny tip of metal at the end of the barrel of my gun, fixed now on this old, tall blind man, utterly at my mercy.

I knew then, how much I wanted to live, to be moving among the beauty and chaos of this universe, how I could not give up, for the sake of some further chaotic event, all the love and peace I had fought for and found. I shivered with life, the sound of the wren was a hymn to the glory of creation, I, too, wanted to be part of it, even if no more than a leaf, a flower, I wanted my place in it, my own place, the establishment of my being. At the same time the most exhausting sense of my own loneliness hit me, and the loneliness of the man before me, amidst the chaos of creation. I wanted to stand up before him and shout

"Here I am! It's me. It's Matthew, Matthew Blake!"

and I wanted him to name himself to me, that's all, introduce himself, here, in this place, now.

I knew the thumping of pain inside my chest; I knew the beating of my heart, and I knew God, in a way never clear to me before. God in place, God in chaos, God in loneliness, God in simply being. God touched me then, for a moment, in the silence, the absence, the sense of loneliness, the chaos, and there was nothing to be done but to dwell in that silence and absence. Every sense in my body was heightened, every cell and nerve and tissue surged with awareness. It was a moment of birth, or a moment of death, I do not know which. But the sense of it has lived with me, making me more aware of quietness, of isolation, of the absence of God, of love.

He had drawn nearer still and I could see that he walked without looking at anything about him; he walked, the stick his eyes. But the expression on his face showed me he was watching inward, the whole world being probed and plotted behind that gaunt, unseeing face.

I forced myself to say it all to my heart again:

"When you aim you must become your target. Take it all in, caress it, be in love with it for just this moment, know its secrets, know where it will hurt most, know from within where it is most vulnerable, imagine its death-wound already delivered, where it is, the open sore, and then touch it, oh so gently, delicately, as a mother will touch the bleeding wound of her child. Do not touch the trigger in anger, never in anger, for at that moment you must touch it with love, or you will miss, pull the trigger with sympathy, with sorrow, above all with love ... "

I picked my spot, right between those eyes. My finger began to press. My whole mind and body began to scream with noise. The moment of intensity had passed almost at once leaving me cold and shaken. He drew closer. Five yards. Four yards. Three.

I could not shoot. Then he was before me, three feet from the rifle; I saw the side of his head, the rim of the hat pressing on his ear, forcing the top of the ear out in an ungainly manner. He sensed something. He stopped. The gun was aiming at his left temple. He did not turn his head. I could shatter his brain into nothing.

"Who's there? Is there anybody there?"

He spoke the words quietly, out of his near darkness into the absolute darkness beyond him. For him the footsteps had mounted the non-existent stairs and the door between him and the intolerable was wide open. I was still. The aches and pain, the trembling, the hesitancy, were gone. I knew. I knew that all the blows a man receives upon his body during his life are nothing to him if only the vision that he has been granted, however impaired and weak, that interior vision by which he lives, remains untainted by untruth. I knew, too, that all my struggles to find my own place were within myself, I was the one I had to face, and no-one else. The man before me, at my mercy, was no different from me. The answer to the question he had asked of the morning, "Who's there? Is there anybody there?" did not matter. There is nobody there; there is you, the person within you you have to cope with, the weight you have to carry as best you can. My finger eased from the trigger. De Valera moved on, more slowly, more cautiously than before.

A great flood of relief came over me and I sighed with the ease I knew. He stopped again and turned his head back towards where I was.

"There is somebody there?" he said, still quietly.

"Yes," I answered him, softly, too, and I removed the cartridge from the rifle and flung it from me into the wood.

"Who are you?" he said.

I came out from the bushes, the rifle held behind me. I did not know how much he could actually see.

"I suppose I must be a ghost who has come close to you and is going from you again, into the darkness."

"I see," he said, and I knew he understood.

"And shall we not shake one another's hands?" he asked me, advancing slowly, his hand outstretched.

I took his hand and knew its brittleness; there was no sense of strength in it at all.

"You're very cold," he said.

"Ghosts are cold."

He took his stick back into his right hand.

"And shall this ghost come back again some day?"

"Not this particular ghost, but no doubt there will be others."

"Very well," he said, his voice suddenly throaty and a little thick. "God bless you, ghost, and God be with you."

He turned away from me and continued his walk, steady, upright, proud. And shaken?

I swung my rifle round my head and let it fly from me into the depths of the shrubbery. I followed the great man, from a distance, watchful for his stepping, and left him when we reached the driveway. He turned back towards the college and I turned left towards the gate. There was one thing more I had to do.

I walked back into Cahir and bought myself a hearty breakfast in the hotel. I ate with relish, there was a joy and release in me I had not known since I had loved Joanne. At ten fifteen I set out again and walked back to the college gates. When the black Ford arrived, immediately after noon, I was sitting on a mound of grass at the side of the road. The driver drew in sharply and flung open the door for me.

"Quick, quick," he shouted. I took my time, walking casually from the grass, crushing a cigarette beneath my foot.

We drove for at least a mile, the driver watching often into the mirror, before he dared to speak.

"Well?" he asked, glancing over at me. "You seem to be in great form!"

"Yes," I said, "a great day, a great day."

"He's dead then, the Chief? You did it?"

"No."

There was silence.

"I changed my mind."

He stayed silent a long time.

"Then you've had it, mate, you're a dead man."

"Yes," I answered, lightly, "I'm a ghost."

I told him to take me at once to Manus Cafferky, that I would report only to him, directly. In Cashel he stopped the car, took the keys with him and went into a hotel to phone. He was there for a long time, glancing out the window of the hotel towards the car. I sat at peace. He came out at last and got back into the car.

"Seems you're going to have to face the Man himself."

"The Man!" I said, laughing. "Well, well, well. The Man and the ghost, face to face. That's something to look forward to."

We said little more for the rest of the journey. We headed out from Cashel, taking the road for Thurles, going north.

Late in the afternoon we passed through the village of Glenbeg and I saw the gateway that leads down to the monastery. Memories, sadness, fears, came flooding through me and passed away again, as if they, too, had found their place inside me, the way a shoal of minnows will come into clear water, waltz for a time, then disappear, together. We drove another few miles and turned onto a narrow stone road leading along by the coast. It began to rain. The wipers on the old car worked noisily. We stopped at a gate and my taciturn companion told me to get out and open it.

"No sir," I answered at once. "I'm here to see the Man, and I'm not getting out in that rain."

He muttered a curse and got out to open the gate himself. We moved in past the pillars; he had to get out again to close the gate behind us. He was wet, and angry. We drove up a narrow laneway, the ground underneath rutted and damp, furze and fuchsia scraping at the window of the car. At the end of the laneway there was a cottage, long and low, two other cars parked outside. I ran to the door and it opened as I reached it. I stepped into the darkness of the kitchen. I waited; gradually my eyes got used to the dimness within.

Manus Cafferky was sitting in a low armchair at the end of the room, to my left. He was watching me, a grin of satisfaction on his face. Standing to my right, inside the door, was another man I did not know; directly opposite the door, his back to a drearily burning fire, stood a squat man, bald and elderly; it was only when he spoke I knew him.

"Well, well, well, Brother Gonzalez!" came the voice filled with mirth and humour.

"Ambrose!" I said, astonished, and a little relieved. "So you're the Man! Who'd ever have thought it?"

He came over to me and shook my hand warmly and firmly as ever. Then he slapped me on the back and brought me to the table in the centre of the room. He motioned to me to sit at one end and then he walked round the table and sat facing me at the other. He was wearing a grey suit, a waistcoat, a tie.

"Well, Ambrose, are you still aspiring to sanctity?" I asked him.

There came that old, familiar chuckle as he leaned forward, his elbows on the table, his plump hands joined.

"Life moves on, Matthew, life moves on. It dawned on the Brothers that I was up to something. I moved away from their doleful God into the world of blood and guts."

"Blood and guts it is, too," I retorted, "from what I've been hearing of the IRA. Blood sacrifice the idea still?"

Again the low, rivulet, chuckle.

"Those you love you hurt the most, Gonzalez, you know that. The law of love, Christ told us, Pearse knew it, so do we. To love you must move heaven and earth, and those we love will see it all one day, I promise you."

"I used to believe that too, one day," I said, "but I have come to know you must not impose your burden on others. Sufficient to each man his burden in life, Ambrose. Our task is to learn to bear our own weight, to come to terms with what is our own individual shape and heaviness in this world, and respect the right of everyone else to name and shoulder their own burdens."

"Ah! the philosopher still, Gonzalez, still the eager, would-be lover. Nothing changes, nothing ever changes."

He sighed and leaned his heavy, round head forward on his joined hands. He looked weary, now, and old, the dim light from the window sending a sheen over the bald meadow of his skull.

"But there's the dream, Matthew," he went on, his voice little more than a whisper, "there's the dream that is the burden we bear, too, the dream that your friend, Eamon de Valera, has turned into a nightmare for us all. That is the law of our love, Matthew, the dream."

"But you have to bear that burden yourself, Ambrose, you must be strong enough for that. If each man can take it upon himself to bear his own weight, without adding to the burden of others ... Christ's dream did not hurt anyone but himself and he bore the weight of that hurt. And of ours."

"Oh ho! theology, too, Matt? well! well! well! And I say to you that Christ said he came, not to bring us peace, but the sword! Now, Matthew Blake, lover, what have you to say to that?"

He sat back, a grin of near-satisfaction on his face.

There was a growl from the corner behind him.

"For fuck's sake get on with it Eamon!"

Ambrose shrugged his shoulders, smiled at me and leaned forward again onto the table.

"Your old friend Manus is growing impatient. There is no philosophy there, Matt, no theology, only the impetus of the dream. A bit hasty, but true at heart. Your name came up between us, Matt, several times ... he told me how you two had fought, how much you hated that man, our tormentor. We thought you were our man for the job, Matt, but we were wrong, we were very definitely wrong!"

"I hate what de Valera has done, Ambrose, I have always despised his machinations, his cunning, his success. But I have seen enough blood-letting to have learned it serves only to keep the old hatreds spinning all the faster. We have seen enough of war, Ambrose, surely we have seen enough of war to know it can never, ever achieve anything. And I have found love, and my place in life, and all I want to do is to go back there and live in quiet with those who share my burdens and whose burdens I can lighten. Can you understand that, Ambrose?"

His hands were tightly clenched; I could see the tufts of grey hair on his fingers, the delicate pink flush of his still smooth skin. He watched me in silence, then he sighed.

"Yes, Matt, sometimes I recall our times of prayer and peace, our talks, our hopes. And sometimes, too, I envy you. I envy you."

Suddenly his hands separated and struck the table a dull thud. He sat back.

"Go home, Matthew Blake, go home! Go back to your place, back to your love, back to your quiet dreams. And whatever God is with you, Matt, I hope he'll keep you in his care. Go! James will drive you back to Westport. Your own car will be there. Your wife, Joanne isn't it, must be getting anxious. Go!"

He was leaning back on the chair, his hands holding the edge of the table. He lowered his head, his gaze fixed on the floor beneath his feet. I stood up, hesitantly.

"We will not meet again, Gonzalez, not in this world."

I was heading around the table to take his hand. Suddenly an angry Manus was on his feet.

"You can't just let him go like that, man," he shouted. "He knows all about us, now. And he let us down, he disobeyed orders. He can't just walk away like that!"

Manus was standing at the table looking down at Ambrose. The old man sighed and waved his arm in a vague gesture of dismissal.

"Matthew will give us his word ... " he began and was interrupted.

"It won't do, Ambrose, it won't do at all!"

Ambrose looked up at me, quietly.

"Matthew, swear to me you will never breathe a word of today's events, ever, that you will bring all you have done and seen and heard today with you to your grave."

I looked down at him. Oh he was tired now, tired and lonely and astray.

"I will not breathe a word about any of it, Ambrose. I swear it."

Ambrose waved his arm again.

"There!" he said, "that's good enough for me. I have reason to know that I can trust your word!"

"Well, it's not good enough for me!" Manus shouted.

"What do you want, Manus? Another sacrifice?"

"I don't care what you call it! I want this man to be punished. I want him silenced. For ever!"

Ambrose turned towards me, wearily.

"Manus wants to impose his burden on you, Matthew. I'm sorry we dragged you into this. It seemed like a good idea ... "

He stood up, slowly, the way an old man rises, reluctantly, from his restplace. But suddenly he moved, with uncanny speed and strength, grasping Manus and shoving him violently back against the wall where he held him, staring straight into his eyes.

"I am sending Matthew home," he enunciated, quietly, "and you will do nothing more about it. Do you hear?"

Manus looked down sullenly at the man who was in every way stronger than he was. Then he looked at me and the hatred in his eyes was unbearable.

"Wait, Ambrose," I said, "I came up here today because there is an unfinished job before me. When Manus appeared out of the night into my life he brought hatred and deceit and murder. He tried to ruin what I had been labouring to build all my life. There is something unfinished between us. I am willing to finish it, right now."

Ambrose grinned and let Manus go.

"Are we talking about a duel?" he asked me.

"Something like that," I answered.

"With pistols? as they used to do in the good old days?"

"With fists, Ambrose. With fists. We began something many years ago, in St Joseph's school, and we were not allowed to finish it. We can finish it now and then I will go home in peace."

There was a broad grin on Manus's face. Immediately he began to take his waistcoat off. I turned and walked resolutely out into the evening. The rain had eased a little but the ground was wet. There was a grassy patch in front of the cottage that would serve. I removed my jacket and waistcoat and handed them to the man who had driven me from Cahir. I rolled up the sleeves of my shirt and walked out onto the patch of grass.

All around the cottage the bushes of furze, fuchsia and rowan trees cut off any view of the world. The rain fell silently and I thought I could hear a murmur from the sea away to the right. I suddenly felt very, very tired. But I stood calmly, shouldering my own weight for the very first time. And then Manus stood in the doorway, Ambrose behind him, and he began to walk slowly towards me. I remembered the yard in Drommasheelin; how the circle spins and spins and spins! Amen! I whispered to myself. Morning and evening, the final circle.

DAVID

THEY CLOSED THE CURTAINS ROUND HIS BED.

Bed number four ...

The sun had shifted away from the window. The afternoon heaviness was beginning to settle in.

We were ushered, gently, from the ward, out into the corridor. Some of us were weeping. In me there has come a heaviness, a burden I did not anticipate. As if the weight of his living and his dying has descended on my shoulders.

His last moments eminently peaceful. Still absent. Unspeaking. Eyes closed. Just once he lifted his hand to his face, as if to wipe something away. Memories? Life? The world? Then he ceased to breathe. Left, as a ghost might leave, who has haunted us a while.

They brought us into a quiet room. Someone has come with a trolley. Tea. Biscuits. There will be phone-calls, arrangements, pain.

One nurse called me aside. Gave me a big, plastic sack. Black.

"His things," she said.

The slim, silver, Parker pen she found in the pocket of his dressing-gown, she gave me that, too.

She pressed my hand, in a kindly way.

"He was a grand man, a grand man."

Then she turned away from me.

"Must go," she said, "must get on now with my rounds."

ON THIS SHORE

They laid him on his back
in the flat-bottomed
ramshackle boat that the dead use
and carried him down to the shore;

quickly he sank
into the current's hold
and did not come up again for air;
when I had kissed his forehead

he was already cold
and had begun to sweat;
soon he will have shed all baggage,
the great gannet of life

will be gliding over him like a dream;
he has cast off at last
from the high white cross
to which he was anchored

and I have turned back,
carrying his burden,
leaving a deeper set of footprints
across the sand.